# SECTOR GENERAL
## WAS DYING

The vast, complex structure dedicated to the relief of suffering and the advance of medicine was succumbing like any terminal patient to a disease too powerful to resist. The patients with their exotic variations of physiology and metabolism, were being evacuated. In dark wards the weird, wonderful fabrications, which constituted alien ideas of comfortable beds, crouched like surreal ghosts along the walls. With the departure of the E-Ts, gone were the strange environments which housed them, the Translators which allowed them to communicate, the knowledge which made it possible for one species to treat another.

For Sector General, the galactic center of healing, was about to be destroyed in an interstellar war!

# STAR SURGEON

**James White**

A Del Rey Book

BALLANTINE BOOKS · NEW YORK

A Del Rey Book
Published by Ballantine Books

ISBN 0-345-29169-7

Manufactured in the United States of America

First Edition: March 1963
Fourth Printing: January 1981

First Canadian Printing: May 1963

Cover art by Dean Ellis

# Chapter One

eÈÈÈÈÈÈÈÈÈÈÈÈÈÈÈÈÈÈÈÈÈÈÈÈÈÈÈÈÈÈÈÈÈÈÈÈÈÈÈÈÈ

FAR OUT on the galactic Rim, where star systems were sparse and the darkness nearly absolute, Sector Twelve General Hospital hung in space. In its three hundred and eighty-four levels were reproduced in the environments of all the intelligent life-forms known to the Galactic Federation, a biological spectrum ranging from the ultra-frigid methane life-forms through the more normal oxygen- and chlorine-breathing types up to the exotic beings who existed by the direct conversion of hard radiation. Its thousands of viewports were constantly ablaze with light—light in the dazzling variety of colour and intensity necessary for the visual equipment of its extra-terrestrial patients and staff—so that to approaching ships the great hospital looked like a tremendous, cylindrical Christmas tree.

Sector General represented a two-fold miracle of engineering and psychology. Its supply and maintenance was handled by the Monitor Corps—the Federation's executive and law enforcement arm—who also saw to its administration, but the traditional friction between the military and civilian members of its staff did not occur. Neither were there any serious squabbles among its ten thousand-odd medical personnel, who were composed of over sixty different life-forms with sixty differing sets of mannerisms, body odours and ways of looking at life. Perhaps their one and only common denominator was the need of all doctors, regardless of size, shape or number of legs, to cure the sick.

The staff of Sector General was a dedicated, but not always serious, group of beings who were fanatically tolerant of all forms of intelligent life—had this not been so they would not have been there in the first place. And they prided themselves that no case was too big, too small or too hopeless. Their advice or assistance was sought by medical authorities from all over the Galaxy. Pacifists all, they waged a constant, all-out war against suffering and disease whether it was in individuals or whole planetary populations.

5

But there were times when the diagnosis and treatment of a diseased interstellar culture, entailing the surgical removal of deeply-rooted prejudice and unsane moral values without either the patient's cooperation or consent could, despite the pacifism of the doctors concerned, lead to the waging of war. Period.

* * *

The patient being brought into the observation ward was a large specimen—about one thousand pounds mass, Conway estimated—and resembled a giant, upright pear. Five thick, tentacular appendages grew from the narrow head section and a heavy apron of muscle at its base gave evidence of a snail-like, although not necessarily slow, method of locomotion. The whole body surface looked raw and lacerated, as though someone had been trying to take its skin off with a wire brush.

To Conway there was nothing very unusual about the physical aspect of the patient or its condition, six years in space Sector General Hospital having accustomed him to much more startling sights, so he moved forward to make a preliminary examination. Immediately the Monitor Corps lieutenant who had accompanied the patient's trolley into the ward moved closer also. Conway tried to ignore the feeling of breath on the back of his neck and took a closer look at the patient.

Five large mouths were situated below the root of each tentacle, four being plentifully supplied with teeth and the fifth housing the vocal apparatus. The tentacles themselves showed a high degree of specialisation at their extremities; three of them were plainly manipulatory, one bore the patient's visual equipment and the remaining member terminated in a horn-tipped, boney mace. The head was featureless, being simply an osseus dome housing the patient's brain.

There wasn't much else to be seen from a superficial examination. Conway turned to get his deep probe gear, and walked on the Monitor officer's feet.

"Have you ever considered taking up medicine seriously, Lieutenant?" he said irritably.

The lieutenant reddened, his face making a horrible clash of colour against the dark green of his uniform collar. He said stiffly, "This patient is a criminal. It was found in circumstances which indicate that it killed and ate the other member of its ship's crew. It has been unconscious during the trip here, but I've been ordered to stand guard on it just in case. I'll try to stay out of your way, Doctor."

Conway swallowed, his eyes going to the vicious-looking, horny bludgeon with which, he had no doubt, the patient's species had battered their way to the top of their evolutionary tree. He said drily, "Don't try too hard, Lieutenant."

Using his eyes and a portable x-ray scanner Conway examined his patient thoroughly inside and out. He took several specimens, including sections of the affected skin, and sent them off to Pathology with three closely-written pages of covering notes. Then he stood back and scratched his head.

The patient was warm-blooded, oxygen-breathing, and had fairly normal gravity and pressure requirements which, when considered with the general shape of the beastie, put its physiological classification as EPLH. It seemed to be suffering from a well-developed and widespread epithelioma, the symptoms being so plain that he really should have begun treatment without waiting for the Path report. But a cancerous skin condition did not, ordinarily, render a patient deeply unconscious.

That could point to psychological complications, he knew, and in that case he would have to call in some specialised help. One of his telepathic colleagues was the obvious choice, if it hadn't been for the fact that telepaths could only rarely work minds that were not already telepathic and of the same species as themselves. Except for the very odd instance, telepathy had been found to be a strictly closed circuit form of communication. Which left his GLNO friend, the empath Dr. Prilicla . . .

Behind him the Lieutenant coughed gently and said, "When you've finished the examination, Doctor, O'Mara would like to see you."

Conway nodded. "I'm going to send someone to keep an eye on the patient," he said, grinning, "guard them as well as you've guarded me."

Going through to the main ward Conway detailed an Earth-human nurse—a very good-looking Earth-human nurse —to duty in the observation ward. He could have sent in one of the Tralthan FGLIs, who belonged to a species with

7

six legs and so built that beside one of them an Earthly elephant would have seemed a fragile, sylph-like creature, but he felt that he owed the Lieutenant something for his earlier bad manners.

Twenty minutes later, after three changes of protective armour and a trip through the chlorine section, a corridor belonging to the AUGL water-breathers and the ultra-refrigerated wards of the methane life-forms, Conway presented himself at the office of Major O'Mara.

As Chief Psychologist of a multi-environment hospital hanging in frigid blackness at the Galactic rim, he was responsible for the mental well-being of a Staff of ten thousand entities who were composed of eighty-seven different species. O'Mara was a very important man at Sector General. He was also, on his own admission, the most approachable man in the hospital. O'Mara was fond of saying that he didn't care who approached him or when, but if they hadn't a very good reason for pestering him with their silly little problems then they needn't expect to get away from him again unscathed. To O'Mara the medical staff were patients, and it was the generally held belief that the high level of stability among that variegated and often touchy bunch of e-ts was due to them being too scared of O'Mara to go mad. But today he was in an almost sociable mood.

"This will take more than five minutes so you'd better sit down, Doctor," he said sourly when Conway stopped before his desk. "I take it you've had a look at our cannibal?"

Conway nodded and sat down. Briefly he outlined his findings with regard to the EPLH patient, including his suspicion that there might be complications of a psychological nature. Ending, he asked, "Do you have any other information on its background, apart from the cannibalism?"

"Very little," said O'Mara. "It was found by a Monitor patrol vessel in a ship which, although undamaged, was broadcasting distress signals. Obviously it became too sick to operate the vessel. There was no other occupant, but because the EPLH was a new species to the rescue party they went over its ship with a fine-tooth comb, and found that there should have been another person aboard. They discovered this through a sort of ship's log cum personal diary kept on tape by the EPLH, and by study of the airlock tell-tales and similar protective gadgetry the details of which don't concern us at the moment. However, all the facts point to there being two entities aboard the ship, and the log tape suggests pretty strongly that the other one came to a sticky end at the hands, and teeth, of your patient."

O'Mara paused to toss a slim sheaf of papers on to his lap and Conway saw that it was a typescript of the relevant sections of the log. He had time only to discover that the EPLH's victim had been the ship's doctor, then O'Mara was talking again.

"We know nothing about its planet of origin," he said morosely, "except that it is somewhere in the other galaxy. However, with only one quarter of our own Galaxy explored, our chances of finding its home world are negligible——"

"How about the Ians," said Conway, "maybe they could help?"

The Ians belonged to a culture originating in the other galaxy which had planted a colony in the same sector of the home galaxy which contained the Hospital. They were an unusual species—classification GKNM—which went into a chrysalis stage at adolescence and metamorphosized from a ten-legged crawler into a beautiful, winged life-form. Conway had had one of them as a patient three months ago. The patient had been long since discharged, but the two GKNM doctors, who had originally come to help Conway with the patient, had remained at Sector General to study and teach.

"A Galaxy's a big place," said O'Mara with an obvious lack of enthusiasm, "but try them by all means. However, to get back to your patient, the biggest problem is going to come *after* you've cured it.

"You see, Doctor," he went on, "this particular beastie was found in circumstances which show pretty conclusively that it is guilty of an act which every intelligent species we know of considers a crime. As the Federation's police force among other things the Monitor Corps is supposed to take certain measures against criminals like this one. They are supposed to be tried, rehabilitated or punished as seems fit. But how can we give this criminal a fair trial when we know nothing at all about its background, a background which just might contain the possibility of extenuating circumstances? At the same time we can't just let it go free..."

"Why not?" said Conway. "Why not point it in the general direction from whence it came and administer a judicial kick in the pants?"

"Or why not let the patient die," O'Mara replied, smiling, "and save trouble all around?"

Conway didn't speak. O'Mara was using an unfair argument and they both knew it, but they also knew that nobody would be able to convince the Monitor enforcement section that curing the sick and punishing the malefactor were not of equal importance in the Scheme of Things.

"What I want you to do," O'Mara resumed, "is to find out all you can about the patient and its background after it comes to and during treatment. Knowing how soft-hearted, or soft-headed you are, I expect you will side with the patient during the cure and appoint yourself an unofficial counsel for the defence. Well, I won't mind that if in so doing you obtain the information which will enable us to summon a jury of its peers. Understood?"

Conway nodded.

O'Mara waited precisely three seconds, then said, "If you've nothing better to do than laze about in that chair . . ."

Immediately on leaving O'Mara's office Conway got in touch with Pathology and asked for the EPLA report to be sent to him before lunch. Then he invited the two Ian GKNMs to lunch and arranged for a consultation with Prilicla regarding the patient shortly afterwards. With these arrangements made he felt free to begin his rounds.

During the two hours which followed Conway had no time to think about his newest patient. He had fifty-three patients currently in his charge together with six doctors in various stages of training and a supporting staff of nurses, the patients and medical staff comprising eleven different physiological types. There were special instruments and procedures for examining these extra-terrestrial patients, and when he was accompanied by a trainee whose pressure and gravity requirements differed both from those of the patient to be examined and himself, then the 'routine' of his rounds could become an extraordinarily complicated business.

But Conway looked at all his patients, even those whose convalescence was well advanced or whose treatment could have been handled by a subordinate. He was well aware that this was a stupid practice which only served to give him a lot of unnecessary work, but the truth was promotion to a resident Senior Physician was still too recent for him to have become used to the large-scale delegation of responsibility. He foolishly kept on trying to do everything himself.

After rounds he was scheduled to give an initial mid-wifery lecture to a class of DBLF nurses. The DBLFs were furry, multipedal beings resembling outsize caterpillars and were native to the planet Kelgia. They also breathed the same atmospheric mixture as himself, which meant that he was able to do without a pressure suit. To this purely physical comfort was added the fact that talking about such elementary stuff as the reason for Kelgian females conceiving only once in their lifetime and then producing quads who were invariably divided equally in sex, did not call for great concentration on his part. It left a large section of his mind free to worry about the alleged cannibal in his observation ward.

## Chapter Two

HALF AN hour later he was with the two Ian doctors in the Hospital's main dining hall—the one which catered for Tralthan, Kelgian, human and the various other warm-blooded, oxygen-breathers on the Staff—eating the inevitable salad. This in itself did not bother Conway unduly, in fact, lettuce was downright appetising compared with some of the things he had had to eat while playing host to other e-t colleagues, but he did not think that he would ever get used to the gale they created during lunch.

The GKNM denizens of Ia were a large, delicate, winged life-form who looked something like a dragonfly. To their rod-like but flexible bodies were attached four insectile legs, manipulators, the usual sensory organs and three tremendous sets of wings. Their table manners were not actually unpleasant—it was just that they did not sit down to dine, they hovered. Apparently eating while in flight aided their digestions as well as being pretty much a conditioned reflex with them.

11

Conway set the Path report on the table and placed the sugar bowl on top of it to keep it from blowing away. He said, " ... You'll see from what I've just been reading to you that this appears to be a fairly simple case. Unusually so, I'd say, because the patient is remarkably clear of harmful bacteria of any type. Its symptoms indicate a form of epithelioma, that and nothing else, which makes its unconsciousness rather puzzling. But maybe some information on its planetary environment, sleeping periods and so on, would clarify things, and that is why I wanted to talk to you.

"We know that the patient comes from your galaxy. Can you tell me anything at all about its background?"

The GKNM on Conway's right drifted a few inches back from the table and said through its Translator, "I'm afraid I have not yet mastered the intricacies of your physiological classification system, Doctor. What does the patient look like?"

"Sorry, I forgot," said Conway. He was about to explain in detail what an EPLH was, then he began sketching on the back of the Path report instead. A few minutes later he held up the result and said, "It looks something like that."

Both Ians dropped to the floor.

Conway who had never known the GKNMs to stop either eating or flying during a meal was impressed by the reaction.

He said, "You know about them, then?"

The GKNM on the right made noises which Conway's Translator reproduced as a series of barks, the e-t equivalent of an attack of stuttering. Finally it said, "We know of them. We have never seen one of them, we do not know their planet of origin, and before this moment we were not sure that they had actual physical existence. They ... they are gods, Doctor."

*Another VIP ... !* though Conway, with a sudden sinking feeling. His experience with VIP patients was that their cases were *never* simple. Even if the patient's condition was nothing serious there were invariably complications, none of which were medical.

"My colleague is being a little too emotional," the other GKNM broke in. Conway had never been able to see any physical difference between the two Ians, but somehow this one had the air of being a more cynical, world-weary dragonfly. "Perhaps I can tell you what little is known, and de-

12

duced, about them rather than enumerate all the things which are not . . ."

The species to which the patient belonged was not a numerous one, the Ian doctor went on to explain, but their sphere of influence in the other galaxy was tremendous. In the social and psychological sciences they were very well advanced, and individually their intelligence and mental capacity was enormous. For reasons known only to themselves they did not seek each other's company very often, and it was unheard of for more than one of them to be found on any planet at the same time for any lengthy period.

They were always the supreme ruler on the worlds they occupied. Sometimes it was a beneficient rule, sometimes harsh—but the harshness, when viewed with a century or so's hindsight, usually turned out to be beneficence in disguise. They used people, whole planetary populations, and even interplanetary cultures, purely as a means to solve the problems which they set themselves, and when the problem was solved they left. At least this was the impression received by not quite unbiased observers.

In a voice made flat and emotionless only because of the process of Translation the Ian went on, ". . . Legends seem to agree that one of them will land on a planet with nothing but its ship and a companion who is always of a different species. By using a combination of defensive science, psychology and sheer business acumen they overcome local prejudice and begin to amass wealth and power. The transition from local authority to absolute planetary rule is gradual, but then they have plenty of time. They are, of course, immortal."

Faintly, Conway heard his fork clattering on to the floor. It was a few minutes before he could steady either his hands or his mind.

There were a few extra-terrestrial species in the Federation who possessed very long life-spans, and most of the medically advanced cultures—Earth's included—had the means of extending life considerably with rejuvenation treatments. Immortality, however, was something they did *not* have, nor had they ever had the chance to study anyone who possessed it. Until now, that was. Now Conway had a patient to care for, and cure and, most of all, investigate. Unless . . .

13

but the GKNM was a doctor, and a doctor would not say immortal if he merely meant long-lived.

"Are you sure?" croaked Conway.

The Ian's answer took a long time because it included the detailing of a great many facts, theories and legends concerning these beings who were satisfied to rule nothing less than a planet apiece. At the end of it Conway was still not sure that his patient was immortal, but everything he had heard seemed to point that way.

Hesitantly, he said, "After what I've just heard perhaps I shouldn't ask, but in your opinion are these beings capable of committing an act of murder and cannibalism—"

"No!" said one Ian.

"Never!" said the other.

There was, of course, no hint of emotion in the Translated replies, but their sheer volume was enough to make everyone in the dining hall look up.

A few minutes later Conway was alone. The Ians had requested permission to see the legendary EPLH and then dashed off full of awe and eagerness. Ians were nice people, Conway thought, but at the same time it was his considered opinion that lettuce was fit only for rabbits. With great firmness he pushed his slightly mussed salad away from him and dialled for steak with double the usual accessories.

This promised to be a long, hard day.

When Conway returned to the observation ward the Ians had gone and the patient's condition was unchanged. The Lieutenant was still guarding the nurse on duty—closely—and was beginning to blush for some reason. Conway nodded gravely, dismissed the nurse and was giving the Path report a rereading when Dr. Prilicla arrived.

Prilicla was a spidery, fragile, low-gravity being of classification GLNO who had to wear G-nullifiers constantly to keep from being mashed flat by a gravity which most other species considered normal. Besides being a very competent doctor Prilicla was the most popular person in the hospital, because its empathic faculty made it nearly impossible for the little being to be disagreeable to anyone. And, although it also possessed a set of large, iridescent wings it sat down at mealtimes and ate spaghetti with a fork. Conway liked Prilicla a lot.

Conway briefly described the EPLH's condition and back-

14

ground as he saw it, then ended, "...I know you can't get much from an unconscious patient, but it would help me if you could—"

"There appears to be a misunderstanding here, Doctor," Prilicla broke in, using the form of words which was the nearest it ever came to telling someone they were wrong. "The patient is conscious..."

*"Get back!"*

Warned as much by Conway's emotional radiation at the thought of what the patient's boney club could do to Prilicla's egg-shell body as his words, the little GLNO skittered backwards out of range. The Lieutenant edged closer, his eyes on the still motionless tentacle which ended in that monstrous bludgeon. For several seconds nobody moved or spoke, while outwardly the patient remained unconscious. Finally Conway looked at Prilicla. He did not have to speak.

Prilicla said, "I detect emotional radiation of a type which emanates only from a mind which is consciously aware of itself. The mental processes themselves seem slow and, considering the physical size of the patient, weak. In detail, it is radiating feelings of danger, helplessness and confusion. There is also an indication of some overall sense of purpose."

Conway sighed.

"So it's playing 'possum," said the Lieutenant grimly, talking mostly to himself.

The fact that the patient was feigning unconsciousness worried Conway less than it did the Corpsman. In spite of the mass of diagnostic equipment available to him he subscribed firmly to the belief that a doctor's best guide to any malfunction was a communicative and co-operative patient. But how did one open a conversation with a being who was a near deity...?

"We...we are going to help you," he said awkwardly. "Do you understand what I'm saying?"

The patient remained motionless as before.

Prilicla said, "There is no indication that it heard you, Doctor."

"But if it's conscious..." Conway began, and ended the sentence with a helpless shrug.

He began assembling his instruments again and with Prilicla's help examined the EPLH again, paying special attention to the organs of sight and hearing. But there was no physical or emotional reaction while the examination was in progress, despite the flashing lights and a considerable amount of ungentle probing. Conway could see no evidence of physical malfunction in any of the sensory organs, yet the patient remained completely unaware of all outside stimulus. Physically it was unconscious, insensible to everything going on around it, except that Prilicla insisted that it wasn't.

*What a crazy, mixed-up demi-god,* thought Conway. Trust O'Mara to send him the weirdies. Aloud he said, "The only explanation I can see for this peculiar state of affairs is that the mind you are receiving has severed or blocked off contact with all its sensory equipment. The patient's condition is not the cause of this, therefore the trouble must have a psychological basis. I'd say the beastie is urgently in need of psychiatric assistance.

"However," he ended, "the head-shrinkers can operate more effectively on a patient who is physically well, so I think we should concentrate on clearing up this skin condition first . . ."

A specific had been developed at the hospital against epithelioma of the type affecting the patient, and Pathology had already stated that it was suited to the EPLH's metabolism and would produce no harmful side-effects. It took only a few minutes for Conway to measure out a test dosage and inject subcutaneously. Prilicla moved up beside him quickly to see the effect. This, they both knew, was one of the rare, rapid-action miracles of medicine—its effect would be apparent in a matter of seconds rather than hours or days.

Ten minutes later nothing at all had happened.

"A tough guy," said Conway, and injected the maximum safe dose.

Almost at once the skin in the area darkened and lost its dry, cracked look. The dark area widened perceptibly as they watched, and one of the tentacles twitched slightly.

"What's its mind doing?" said Conway.

"Much the same as before," Prilicla replied, "but with mounting anxiety apparent since the last injection. I detect feelings of a mind trying to make a decision . . . of making a decision . . ."

Prilicla began to tremble violently, a clear sign that the emotional radiation of the patient had intensified. Conway had his mouth open to put a question when a sharp, tearing sound dragged his attention back to the patient. The EPLH was heaving and throwing itself against its restraining har-

16

ness. Two of the anchoring straps had parted and it had worked a tentacle free. The one with the club . . .

Conway ducked frantically, and avoided having his head knocked off by a fraction of an inch—he felt that ultimate in blunt instruments actually touch his hair. But the Lieutenant was not so lucky. At almost the end of its swing the boney mace thudded into his shoulder, throwing him across the tiny ward so hard that he almost bounced off the wall. Prilicla, with whom cowardice was a prime survival characteristic, was already clinging with its sucker-tipped legs to the ceiling, which was the only safe spot in the room.

From his position flat on the floor Conway heard other straps go and saw two more tentacles begin feeling about. He knew that in a few minutes the patient would be completely free of the harness and able to move about the room at will. He scrambled quickly to his knees, crouched, then dived for the berserk EPLH. As he hung on tightly with his arms around its body just below the roots of the tentacles Conway was nearly deafened by a series of barking roars coming from the speaking orifice beside his ear. The noise translated as "Help me! Help me!" Simultaneously he saw the tentacle with the great, boney bludgeon at its tip swing downwards. There was a crash and a three inch hollow appeared on the floor at the point where he had been lying a few seconds previously.

Tackling the patient the way he had done might have seemed foolhardy, but Conway had been trying to keep his head in more ways than one. Clinging tightly to the EPLH's body below the level of those madly swinging tentacles, Conway knew, was the next safest place in the room.

Then he saw the Lieutenant . . .

The Lieutenant had his back to the wall, half lying and half sitting up. One arm hung loosely at his side and in the other hand he held his gun, steadying it between his knees, and one eye was closed in a diabolical wink while the other sighted along the barrel. Conway shouted desperately for him to wait, but the noise from the patient drowned him out. At every instant Conway expected the flash and shock of exploding bullets. He felt paralysed with fear, he couldn't even let go.

Then suddenly it was all over. The patient slumped on to its side, twitched and became motionless. Holstering his unfired weapon the Lieutenant struggled to his feet. Conway extricated himself and Prilicla came down off the ceiling.

Awkwardly, Conway said, "Uh, I suppose you couldn't shoot with me hanging on there?"

The Lieutenant shook his head. "I'm a good shot, Doctor, I could have hit it and missed you all right. But it kept shouting "Help me" all the time. That sort of thing cramps a man's style . . ."

# Chapter Three

It was some twenty minutes later, after Prilicla had sent the Lieutenant away to have a cracked humerus set and Conway and the GLNO were fitting the patient with a much stronger harness, that they noticed the absence of the darker patch of skin. The patient's condition was now exactly the same as it had been before undergoing treatment. Apparently the hefty shot which Conway had administered had had only a temporary effect, and that was decidedly peculiar. It was in fact downright impossible.

From the moment Prilicla's empathetic faculty had been brought to bear on the case Conway had been sure that the root of the trouble was psychological. He also knew that a severely warped mind could do tremendous damage to the body which housed it. But this damage was on a purely physical level and its method of repair—the treatment developed and proved time and time again by Pathology—was a hard, physical fact also. And no mind, regardless of its power or degree of malfunction, should be able to ignore, to completely negate, a physical fact. The Universe had, after all, certain fixed laws.

So far as Conway could see there were only two possible explanations. Either the rules were being ignored because the Being who had made them had also the right to ignore them or somehow, someone—or some combination of circumstances or mis-read data—was pulling a fast one. Conway infinitely preferred the second theory because the first one was altogether too shattering to consider seriously. He desperately wanted to go on thinking of his patient with a small P . . .

Nevertheless, when he left the ward Conway paid a visit to the office of Captain Bryson, the Monitor Corps Chaplain, and consulted that officer at some length in a semi-professional capacity—Conway believed in carrying plenty of insurance. His next call was on Colonel Skempton, the officer in charge of Supply, Maintenance and Communications at the Hospital. There he requested complete copies of the patient's log—not just the sections relevant to the murder—together with any other background data available to be sent to his room. Then he went to the AUGL theatre to demonstrate operative techniques on submarine life-forms, and before dinner he was able to work in two hours in the Pathology department during which he discovered quite a lot about his patient's immortality.

When he returned to his room there was a pile of typescript on his desk that was nearly two inches thick. Conway groaned, thinking of his six-hour recreation period and how he was going to spend it. The thought obtruded of how he would have *liked* to spend it, bringing with it a vivid picture of the very efficient and impossibly beautiful Nurse Murchison whom he had been dating regularly of late. But Murchison was currently with the FGLI Maternity Section and their free periods would not coincide for another two weeks.

In the present circumstances perhaps it was just as well, Conway thought, as he settled down for a good long read.

The Corpsmen who had examined the patient's ship had been unable to convert the EPLH's time units into the Earth-human scale with any accuracy, but they had been able to state quite definitely that many of the taped logs were several centuries old and a few of them dated back to two thousand years or more. Conway began with the oldest and sifted carefully through them until he came to the most recent. He discovered almost at once that they were not so much a series of taped diaries—the references to personal items were relatively rare—as a catalogue of memoranda, most of which was highly technical and very heavy going. The data relevant to the murder, which he studied last, was much more dramatic.

*. . . My physician is making me sick,* the final entry read, *it is killing me. I must do something. It is a bad physician for allowing me to become ill. Somehow I must get rid of it . . .*

Conway replaced the last sheet on its pile, sighed, and prepared to adopt a position more conducive to creative thinking; i.e. with his chair tipped far back, feet on desk and practically sitting on the back of his neck.

*What a mess,* he thought.

The separate pieces of the puzzle—or most of them, anyway—were available to him now and required only to be fitted together. There was the patient's condition, not serious so far as the Hospital was concerned but definitely lethal if not treated. Then there was the data supplied by the two Ians regarding this God-like, power-hungry but essentially beneficent race and the companions—who were never of the same species—who always travelled or lived with them. These companions were subject to replacement because they grew old and died while the EPLHs did not. There were also the Path reports, both the first written one he had received before lunch and the later verbal one furnished during his two hours with Thornnastor, the FGLI Diagnostician-in-Charge of Pathology. It was Thornnastor's considered opinion that the EPLH patient was not a true immortal, and the Considered Opinion of a Diagnostician was as near to being a rock-hard certainty as made no difference. But while immortality had been ruled out for various physiological reasons, the tests had shown evidence of longevity or rejuvenation treatments of the unselective type.

Finally there had been the emotion readings furnished by Prilicla before and during their attempted treatment of the patient's skin condition. Prilicla had reported a steady radiation pattern of confusion, anxiety and helplessness. But when the EPLH had received its second injection it had gone berserk, and the blast of emotion exploding from its mind had, in Prilicla's own words, nearly fried the little empath's brains in their own ichor. Prilicla had been unable to get a detailed reading on such a violent eruption of emotion, mainly because it had been tuned to the earlier and more gentle level on which the patient had been radiating, but it agreed that there was evidence of instability of the schizoid type.

20

Conway wriggled deeper into his chair, closed his eyes and let the pieces of the puzzle slide gently into place.

It had begun on the planet where the EPLHs had been the dominant life-form. In the course of time they had achieved civilisation which included interstellar flight and an advanced medical science. Their life-span, lengthy to begin with, was artificially extended so that a relatively short-lived species like the Ians could be forgiven for believing them to be immortal. But a high price had had to be paid for their longevity: reproduction of their kind, the normal urge towards immortality of race in a species of mortal individuals, would have been the first thing to go; then their civilisation would have dissolved—been forced apart, rather—into a mass of star-travelling, rugged individualists, and finally there would have been the psychological rot which set in when the risk of purely physical deterioration had gone.

Poor demi-gods, thought Conway.

They avoided each other's company for the simple reason that they'd already had too much of it—century after century of each other's mannerisms, habits of speech, opinions and the sheer, utter boredom of looking at each other. They had set themselves vast, sociological problems—taking charge of backward or errant planetary cultures and dragging them up by their bootstraps, and similar large-scale philanthropies —because they had tremendous minds, they had plenty of time, they had constantly to fight against boredom and because basically they must have been nice people. And because part of the price of such longevity was an ever-growing fear of death, they had to have their own personal physicians—no doubt the most efficient practitioners of medicine known to them—constantly in attendance.

Only one piece of the puzzle refused to fit and that was the odd way in which the EPLH had negated his attempts to treat it, but Conway had no doubt that that was a physiological detail which would soon become clear as well. The important thing was that he now knew how to proceed.

Not every condition responded to medication, despite Thornnastor's claims to the contrary, and he would have seen that surgery was indicated in the EPLH's case if the whole business had not been so be-fogged with considerations of who and what the patient was and what it was supposed to have done. The fact that the patient was a

21

near-diety, a murderer and generally the type of being not to be trifled with were details which should not have concerned him.

Conway sighed and swung his feet to the floor. He was beginning to feel so comfortable that he decided he had better go to bed before he fell asleep.

Immediately after breakfast next day Conway began setting up things for the EPLH's operation. He ordered the necessary instruments and equipment sent to the observation ward, gave detailed instructions regarding its sterilisation—the patient was supposed to have killed one doctor already for allowing it to become sick, and a dim view would be taken if another one was the cause of it catching something else because of faulty aseptic procedures—and requested the assistance of a Tralthan surgeon to help with the fine work. Then half an hour before he was due to start Conway called on O'Mara.

The Chief Psychologist listened to his report and intended course of action without comment until he had finished, then he said, "Conway, do you realise what could happen to this hospital if that thing got loose? And not just physically loose, I mean. It is seriously disturbed mentally, you say, if not downright psychotic. At the moment it is unconscious, but from what you tell me its grasp of the psychological sciences is such that it could have us eating out of its manipulatory appendage just by talking at us.

"I'm concerned as to what may happen when it wakes up."

It was the first time Conway had heard O'Mara confess to being worried about anything. Several years back when a runaway spaceship had crashed into the hospital, spreading havoc and confusion through sixteen levels, it was said that Major O'Mara had expressed a feeling of concern on that occasion also . . .

"I'm trying not to think about that," said Conway apologetically. "It just confuses the issue."

O'Mara took a deep breath and let it out slowly through his nose, a mannerism of his which could convey more than twenty scathing sentences. He said coldly, "Somebody should think about these things, Doctor. I trust you will have no objection to *me* observing the coming operation . . . ?"

To what was nothing less than a politely worded order there could be no reply other than an equally polite, "Glad to have you, sir."

When they arrived in the observation ward the patient's 'bed' had been raised to a comfortable operating height and the EPLH itself was strapped securely into position. The Tralthan had taken its place beside the recording and anaesthetizing gear and had one eye on the patient, one on its equipment and the other two directed towards Prilicla with whom it was discussing a particularly juicy piece of scandal which had come to light the previous day. As the two beings concerned were PVSJ chlore-breathers the affair could have only an academic interest for them, but apparently their academic interest was intense. At the sight of O'Mara, however, the scandal-mongering ceased forthwith. Conway gave the signal to begin.

The anaesthetic was one of several which Pathology had pronounced safe for the EPLH life-form, and while it was being administered Conway found his mind going off at a tangent towards his Tralthan assistant.

Surgeons of that species were really two beings instead of one, a combination of FGLI and OTSB. Clinging to the leathery back of the lumbering, elephantine Tralthan was a diminutive and nearly mindless being who lived in symbiosis with it. At first glance the OTSB looked like a furry ball with a long ponytail sprouting from it, but a closer look showed that the ponytail was composed of scores of fine manipulators most of which incorporated sensitive visual organs. Because of the *rapport* which existed between the Tralthan and its symbiote the FGLI-OTSB combination were the finest surgeons in the Galaxy. Not all Tralthans chose to link up with a symbiote, but FGLI medics wore them like a badge of office.

Suddenly the OTSB scurried along its host's back and huddled atop the dome-like head between the eye-stalks, its tail hanging down towards the patient and fanning out stiffly. The Tralthan was ready to begin.

"You will observe that this is a surface condition only," Conway said, for the benefit of the recording equipment, "and that the whole skin area looks dead, dried-up and on the point of flaking off. During the removal of the first skin samples no difficulty was encountered, but later specimens resisted removal to a certain extent and the reason was discovered to be a tiny rootlet, approximately one quarter of an inch long and invisible to the naked eye. My naked

23

eye, that is. So it seems clear that the condition is about to enter a new phase. The disease is beginning to dig in rather than remain on the surface, and the more promptly we act the better."

Conway gave the reference numbers of the Path reports and his own preliminary notes on the case, then went on, "...As the patient, for reasons which are at the moment unclear, does not respond to medication I propose surgical removal of the affected tissue, irrigation, cleansing and replacement with surrogate skin. A Tralthan-guided OTSB will be used to insure that the rootlets are also excised. Except for the considerable area to be covered, which will make this a long job, the procedure is straightforward—"

"Excuse me, Doctors," Prilicla broke in, "the patient is still conscious."

An argument, polite only on Prilicla's side, broke out between the Tralthan and the little empath. Prilicla held that the EPLH was thinking thoughts and radiating emotions and the other maintained that it had enough of the anaesthetic in its system to render it completely insensible to everything for at least six hours. Conway broke in just as the argument was becoming personal.

"We've had this trouble before," he said irritably. "The patient has been physically unconscious except for a few minutes yesterday, since its arrival, yet Prilicla detected the presence of rational thought processes. Now the same effect is present while it is under anaesthetic. I don't know how to explain this, it will probably require a surgical investigation of its brain structure to do so, and that is something which will have to wait. The important thing at the moment is that it is physically incapable of movement or of feeling pain. Now shall we begin?"

To Prilicla he added, "Keep listening just in case ..."

# Chapter Four

FOR ABOUT twenty minutes they worked in silence, although the procedure did not require a high degree of concentration. It was rather like weeding a garden, except that everything which grew was a weed and had to be removed one plant at a time. He would peel back an affected area of skin, the OTSB's hair-thin appendages would investigate, probe and detach the rootlets, and he would peel back another tiny segment. Conway was looking forward to the most tedious operation of his career.

Prilicla said, "I detect increasing anxiety linked with a strengthening sense of purpose. The anxiety is becoming intense . . ."

Conway grunted. He could think of no other comment to make.

Five minutes later the Tralthan said, "We will have to slow down, Doctor. We are at a section where the roots are much deeper . . ."

Two minutes later Conway said, "But I can *see* them! How deep are they now?"

"Four inches," replied the Tralthan. "And Doctor, they are visibly lengthening as we work."

"But that's impossible!" Conway burst out; then, "We'll move to another area."

He felt the sweat begin to trickle down his forehead and just beside him Prilicla's gangling, fragile body began to quiver—but not at anything the patient was thinking. Conway's own emotional radiation just then was not a pleasant thing, because in the new area and in the two chosen at random after that the result was the same. Roots from the flaking pieces of skin were burrowing deeper as they watched.

"Withdraw," said Conway harshly.

For a long time nobody spoke. Prilicla was shaking as if a high wind was blowing in the ward. The Tralthan was fussing with its equipment, all four of its eyes focussed on one unimportant knob. O'Mara was looking intently at Conway, also calculatingly and with a large amount of sympathy in his steady grey eyes. The sympathy was because he could recognise when a man was genuinely in a spot and the calculation was due to his trying to work out whether the trouble was Conway's fault or not.

"What happened, Doctor?" he said gently.

Conway shook his head angrily. "I don't know. Yesterday the patient did not respond to medication, today it won't respond to surgery. It's reactions to anything we try to do for it are crazy, impossible! And now our attempt to relieve

25

its condition surgically has triggered off—something—which will send those roots deep enough to penetrate vital organs in a matter of minutes if their present rate of growth is maintained, and you know what that means . . ."

"The patient's sense of anxiety is diminishing," Prilicla reported. "It is still engaged in purposeful thinking."

The Tralthan joined in then. It said, "I have noticed a peculiar fact about those root-like tendrils which join the diseased flakes of skin with the body. My symbiote has extremely sensitive vision, you will understand, and it reports that the tendrils seem to be rooted at each end, so that it is impossible to tell whether the growth is attacking the body or the body is deliberately holding on to the growth."

Conway shook his head distractedly. The case was full of mad contradictions and outright impossibilities. To begin with no patient, no matter how fouled up mentally, should be able to negate the effects of a drug powerful enough to bring about a complete cure within half an hour, and all within a few minutes. And the natural order of things was for a being with a diseased area of skin to slough it off and replace it with new tissue, not hang on to it grimly no matter what. It was a baffling, hopeless case.

Yet when the patient had arrived it had seemed a simple, straightforward case—Conway had felt more concern regarding the patient's background than its condition, whose cure he had considered a routine matter. But somewhere along the way he had missed something, Conway was sure, and because of this sin of omission the patient would probably die during the next few hours. Maybe he had made a snap diagnosis, been too sure of himself, been criminally careless.

It was pretty horrible to lose a patient at any time, and at Sector General losing a patient was an extremely rare occurrence. But to lose one whose condition no hospital anywhere in the civilised galaxy would have considered as being serious . . . Conway swore luridly, but stopped because he hadn't the words to describe how he felt about himself.

"Take it easy, son."

That was O'Mara, squeezing his arm and talking like a father. Normally O'Mara was a bad-tempered, bull-voiced and unapproachable tyrant who, when one went to him for help, sat making sarcastic remarks while the person concerned squirmed and shamefacedly solved his own problems. His

26

present uncharacteristic behaviour proved something, Conway thought bitterly. It proved that Conway had a problem which Conway could not solve himself.

But in O'Mara's expression there was something more than just concern for Conway, and it was probably that deep down the psychologist was a little glad that things had turned out as they did. Conway meant no reflection on O'Mara's character, because he knew that if the Major had been in his position he would have tried as hard if not harder to cure the patient, and would have felt just as badly about the outcome. But at the same time the Chief Psychologist must have been desperately worried about the possibility of a being of great and unknown powers, who was also mentally unbalanced, being turned loose on the Hospital. In addition O'Mara might also be wondering if, beside a conscious and alive EPLH, he would look like a small and untutored boy . . .

"Let's try taking it from the top again," O'Mara said, breaking in on his thoughts. "Is there anything you've found in the patient's background that might point to it wanting to destroy itself?"

"*No!*" said Conway vehemently. "To the contrary! It would want desperately to live. It was taking unselective rejuvenation treatments, which means that the complete cell-structure of its body was regenerated periodically. As the process of storing memory is a product of ageing in the brain cells, this would practically wipe its mind clean after every treatment . . ."

"That's why those taped logs resembled technical memoranda," O'Mara put in. "That's exactly what they were. Still, I prefer our own method of rejuvenation even though we won't live so long, regenerating damaged organs only and allowing the brain to remain untouched . . ."

"I know," Conway broke in, wondering why the usually taciturn O'Mara had become so talkative. Was he trying to simplify the problem by making him state it in non-professional terms? "But the effect of continued longevity treatments, as you know yourself, is to give the possessor an increasing fear of dying. Despite loneliness, boredom and an altogether unnatural existence, the fear grows steadily with the passage of time. That is why it always travelled with its own private physician, it was desperately afraid of sickness

27

or an accident befalling it between treatments, and that is why I can sympathise to a certain extent with its feelings when the doctor who was supposed to keep it well allowed it to get sick, although the business of eating it afterwards—"

"So you are on its side," said O'Mara drily.

"It could make a good plea of self-defence," Conway retorted. "But I was saying that it was desperately afraid of dying, so that it would be constantly trying to get a better, more efficient doctor for itself . . . Oh!"

"Oh, what?" said O'Mara.

It was Prilicla, the emotion sensitive who replied. It said, "Doctor Conway has just had an idea."

"What is it, you young whelp? There's no need to be so damn secretive . . !" O'Mara's voice had lost its gentle fatherly tone, and there was a gleam in his eye which said that he was glad that gentleness was no longer necessary. "What *is* wrong with the patient?"

Feeling happy and excited and at the same time very much unsure of himself, Conway stumbled across to the intercom and ordered some very unusual equipment, checked again that the patient was so thoroughly strapped down that it would be unable to move a muscle, then he said, "My guess is that the patient is perfectly sane and we've been blinding ourselves with psychological red herrings. Basically, the trouble is something it ate."

"I had a bet with myself you would say that sometime during this case," said O'Mara. He looked sick.

The equipment arrived—a slender, pointed wooden stake and a mechanism which would drive it downwards at any required angle and controlled speeds. With the Tralthan's help Conway set it up and moved it into position. He chose a part of the patient's body which contained several vital organs which were, however, protected by nearly six inches of musculature and adipose, then he set the stake in motion. It was just touching the skin and descending at the rate of approximately two inches per hour.

"What the blazes is going on?" stormed O'Mara. "Do you think the patient is a vampire or something!"

"Of course not," Conway replied. "I'm using a wooden stake to give the patient a better chance of defending itself. You wouldn't expect it to stop a steel one, would you." He motioned the Tralthan forward and together they watched the area where the stake was entering the EPLH's body. Every few minutes Prilicla reported on the emotional radiation. O'Mara paced up and down, occasionally muttering to himself.

The point had penetrated almost a quarter of an inch when Conway noticed the first coarsening and thickening of the skin. It was taking place in a roughly circular area, about four inches in diameter, whose centre was the wound created by the stake. Conway's scanner showed a spongy, fibrous growth forming under the skin to a depth of half an inch. Visibly the growth thickened and grew opaque to his scanner's current setting, and within ten minutes it had become a hard, boney plate. The stake had begun to bend alarmingly and was on the point of snapping.

"I'd say the defences are now concentrated at this one point," Conway said, trying to keep his voice steady, "so we'd better have it out."

Conway and the Tralthan rapidly incised around and undercut the newly-formed bony plate, which was immediately transferred into a sterile, covered receptacle. Quickly preparing a shot—a not quite maximum dose of the specific he had tried the previous day—Conway injected, then went back to helping the Tralthan with the repair work on the wound. This was routine work and took about fifteen minutes, and when it was finished there could be no doubt at all that the patient was responding favourably to treatment.

Over the congratulations of the Tralthan and the horrible threats of O'Mara—the Chief Psychologist wanted some questions answered, fast—Prilicla said, "You have effected a cure, Doctor, but the patient's anxiety level has markedly increased. It is almost frantic."

Conway shook his head, grinning. "The patient is heavily anaestheticised and cannot feel anything. However, I agree that at this present moment ..." He nodded towards the sterile container. "... its personal physician must be feeling pretty bad."

In the container the excised bone had begun to soften and leak a faintly purplish liquid. The liquid was rippling and sloshing gently about at the bottom of the container as if it had a mind of its own. Which was, in fact, the case ...


Conway was in O'Mara's office winding up his report on

29

the EPLH and the Major was being highly complimentary in a language which at times made the compliments indistinguishable from insults. But this was O'Mara's way, Conway was beginning to realise, and the Chief Psychologist was polite and sympathetic only when he was professionally concerned about a person.

He was still asking questions.

". . . An intelligent, amoebic life-form, a organised collection of submicroscopic, virus-type cells, would make the most efficient doctor obtainable," said Conway in reply to one of them. "It would reside within its patient and, given the necessary data, control any disease or organic malfunction from the inside. To a being who is pathologically afraid of dying it must have seemed perfect. And it was, too, because the trouble which developed was not really the doctor's fault. It came about through the patient's ignorance of its own physiological background.

"The way I see it," Conway went on, "the patient had been taking its rejuvenation treatments at an early stage of its biological life-time. I mean that it did not wait until middle or old age before regenrating itself. But on this occasion, either because it forgot or was careless or had been working on a problem which took longer than usual, it aged more than it had previously and acquired this skin condition. Pathology says that this was probably a common complaint with this race, and the normal course would be for the EPLH to slough off the affected skin and carry on as usual. But our patient, because the type of its rejuvenation treatment caused memory damage, did not know this, so its personal physician did not know it either."

Conway continued, "This, er, resident physician knew very little about the medical background of its patient-host's body, but its motto must have been to maintain the *status quo* at all costs. When pieces of its patient's body threatened to break away it held on to them, not realising that this could have been a normal occurrence like losing hair or a reptile periodically shedding its skin, especially as its master would have insisted that the occurrence was not natural. A pretty fierce struggle must have developed between the patient's body processes and its Doctor, with the patient's mind also ranged against its doctor. Because of this the doctor had to render the patient unconscious the better to do what it considered to be the right thing.

"When we gave it the test shots the doctor neutralised them. They were a foreign substance being introduced into its patient's body, you see. And you know what happened when we tried surgical removal. It was only when we threatened underlying vital organs with that stake, forcing the doctor to defend its patient at that one point . . ."

"When you began asking for wooden stakes," said O'Mara drily, "I thought of putting *you* in a tight harness."

Conway grinned. He said, "I'm recommending that the EPLH takes his doctor back. Now that Pathology has given it a fuller understanding of its employer's medical and physiological history it should be the ultimate in personal physicians, and the EPLH is smart enough to see that."

O'Mara smiled in return. "And I was worried about what it might do when it became conscious. But it turned out to be a very friendly, likeable type. Quite charming, in fact."

As Conway rose and turned to go he said slyly, "That's because it's such a good psychologist. It is pleasant to people *all* the time . . ."

He managed to get the door shut behind him before the explosion.

## Chapter Five

IN TIME the EPLH patient, whose name was Lonvellin, was discharged and the steady procession of ailing e-ts who came under his care made the memory of Lonvellin's fade in Conway's mind. He did not know whether the EPLH had returned to its home galaxy or was still wandering this one in search of good deeds to do, and he was being kept too busy to care either way. But Conway was not quite finished with the EPLH.

Or more accurately, Lonvellin was not quite finished with Conway . . .

"How would you like to get away from the hospital for a few months, Doctor?" O'Mara said, when Conway had presented himself in the Chief Psychologist's office in answer to an urgent summons over the PA. "It would be in the nature of a holiday, almost."

Conway felt his initial unease grow rapidly into panic. He had urgent personal reasons for *not* leaving the hospital for a few months. He said, "Well . . ."

The psychologist raised his head and fixed Conway with a pair of level grey eyes which saw so much and which opened into a mind so keenly analytical that together they gave O'Mara what amounted to a telepathic faculty. He said drily, "Don't bother to thank me, it is your own fault for curing such powerful, influential patients."

He went on briskly, "This is a large assignment, Doctor, but it will consist mainly of clerical work. Normally it would be given to someone at Diagnostician level, but that EPLH, Lonvellin, has been at work on a planet which it says is urgently in need of medical aid. Lonvellin has requested Monitor Corps as well as hospital assistance in this, and has asked that you personally should direct the medical side. Apparently a Great Intellect isn't needed for the job, just one with a peculiar way of looking at things . . ."

"You're too kind, sir," said Conway.

Grinning, O'Mara said, "I've told you before, I'm here to shrink heads, not inflate them. And now, this is the report on the situation there at the moment . . ." He slid the file he had been reading across to Conway, and stood up. ". . . You can brief yourself on it when you board ship. Be at Lock Sixteen to board *Vespasian* at 2130, meanwhile I expect you have loose ends to tidy up. And Conway, try not to look as if all your relatives had died. Very probably she'll wait for you. If she doesn't, why you have two hundred and seventeen other female DBDGs to chase after. Good-bye and good luck, Doctor."

Outside O'Mara's office Conway tried to work out how best to tidy up his loose ends in the six hours remaining before embarkation time. He was scheduled to take a group of trainees through a basic orientation lecture in ten minutes from now, and it was too late to foist that job onto someone else. That would kill three of the six hours, four if he was unlucky and today he felt unlucky. Then an hour to tape instructions regarding his more serious ward patients, then dinner. He might just do it. Conway began hurrying towards Lock Seven on the one hundred and eighth level.

He arrived at the lock antechamber just as the inner seal

was opening, and while catching his breath began mentally checking off the trainees who were filing past him. Two Kelgian DBLFs who undulated past like giant, silver-furred caterpillars; then a PVSJ from Illensa, the outlines of its spiny, membranous body softened by the chlorine fog inside its protective envelope; a water-breathing Creppelian octopoid, classification AMSL, whose suit made loud bubbling noises. These were followed by five AACPs, a race whose remote ancestors had been a species of mobile vegetable. They were slow moving, but the $CO_2$ tanks which they wore seemed to be the only protection they needed. Then another Kelgian . . .

When they were all inside and the seal closed behind them Conway spoke. Quite unnecessarily and simply as a means of breaking the conversational ice, he said, "Is everyone present?"

Inevitably they all replied in chorus, sending Conway's Translator into a howl of oscillation. Sighing, he began the customary procedure of introducing himself and bidding his new colleagues welcome. It was only at the end of these polite formalities that he worked in a gentle reminder regarding the operating principles of the Translator, and the advisability of speaking one at a time so as not to overload it . . .

On their home worlds these were all very important people, medically speaking. It was only at Sector General that they were new boys, and for some of them the transition from acknowledged master to lowly pupil might be difficult, so that large quantities of tact were necessary when handling them at this stage. Later, however, when they began to settle in, they could be bawled out for their mistakes like anyone else.

"I propose to start our tour at Reception," Conway went on, "where the problems of admittance and initial treatment are dealt with. Then, providing the environment does not require complex protective arrangements for ourselves and the patient's condition is not critical, we will visit the adjacent wards to observe examination procedures on newly-arrived patients. If anyone wants to ask questions at any time, feel free to do so.

"On the way to Reception," he continued, "we will use corridors which may be crowded. There is a complicated system of precedence governing the rights of way of junior and senior medical staff, a system which you will learn in time. But for the present there is just one simple rule to remember. If the being coming at you is bigger than you are, get out of its way."

He was about to add that no doctor in Sector General would *deliberately* trample a colleague to death, but thought better of it. A great many e-ts did not have a sense of humour and such a harmless pleasantry, if taken literally, could lead to endless complications. Instead he said, "Follow me, please."

Conway arranged for the five AACPs, who were the slowest-moving of the group, to follow himself and set the pace for the others. After them came the two Kelgians whose undulating gait was only slightly faster than the vegetable life-forms preceding them. The Chlorine-breather came next and the Creppelian octopoid brought up the rear, the bubbling noise from its suit giving Conway an audible indication that his fifty-yard long tail was all in one piece.

Strung out as they were there was no point in Conway trying to talk, and they negotiated the first stage of the journey in silence—three ascending ramps and a couple of hundred yards of straight and angled corridors. The only person they met coming in the opposite direction was a Nidian wearing the arm-band of a two-year intern. Nidians averaged four feet in height so that nobody was in any danger of being trampled to death. They reached the internal lock which gave access to the water-breather's section.

In the adjoining dressing room Conway supervised the suiting-up of the two Kelgians, then climbed into a lightweight suit himself. The AACPs said that their vegetable metabolism enabled them to exist under water for long periods without protection. The Illensan was already sealed against the oxygen-laden air so that the equally poisonous water did not worry it. But the Creppelian was a water-breather and wanted to take its suit off—it had eight legs which badly needed stretching, it said. But Conway vetoed this on the grounds that it would only be in the water for fifteen minutes at most.

The lock opened into the main AUGL ward, a vast, shadowy tank of tepid green water two hundred feet deep and five hundred feet across. Conway quickly discovered that moving the trainees from the lock to the corridor entrance on the other side was like trying to drive a three dimensional herd of cattle through green glue. With the single exception of the Creppelian they all lost their sense of direction in the water within the first few minutes. Conway had to swim frantically around them, gesticulating and shouting directions, and despite the cooling and drying elements in his suit the interior soon became like an overheated turkish bath. Several times he lost his temper and directed his charges to a place other than the corridor entrance.

And during one particularly chaotic moment an AUGL patient—one of the forty-foot, armoured, fish-like natives of Chalderescol II—swam ponderously towards them. It closed to within five yards, causing a near-panic among the AACPs, said "Student!" and swam away again. Chalders were notoriously antisocial during convalescence, but the incident did not help Conway's temper any.

It seemed much longer than fifteen minutes later when they were assembled in the corridor at the other side of the tank. Conway said, "Three hundred yards along this corridor is the transfer lock into the oxygen section of Reception, which is the best place to see what is going on there. Those of you who are wearing protection against water only will remove their suits, the others will go straight through . . ."

As he was swimming with them towards the lock the Creppelian said to one of the AACPs, "Ours is supposed to be filled with superheated steam, but you have to have done something very bad to be sent there." To which the AACP replied, "Our Hell is hot, too, but there is no moisture in it at all . . ."

Conway had been about to apologise for losing his temper back in the tank, fearing that he might have hurt some sensitive extra-terrestrial feelings, but obviously they hadn't taken what he'd said very seriously.

## Chapter Six

THROUGH THE transparent wall of its observation gallery, Reception showed as a large, shadowy room containing three large control desks, only one of which was currently occupied. The being seated before it was another Nidian, a small, humanoid with seven-fingered hands and an overall coat of tight, curly red fur. Indicator lights on the desk showed that it had just made contact with a ship approaching the hospital.

Conway said, "Listen . . ."

"Identify yourself, please," said the red teddybear in its staccato, barking speech—which was filtered through Conway's Translator as flat, toneless English and which came to the others as equally toneless Kelgian, Illensan or whatever. "Patient, visitor or staff, and species?"

"Pilot, with one passenger-patient aboard," came the reply. "Both human."

There was a short pause, then; "Give your physiological classification, please, or make full-vision contact," said the Nidian with a very Earth-human wink towards the watchers in the gallery. "All intelligent races refer to their own species as human and think of all others as being non-human. What you call yourself has no meaning so far as preparing accommodation for the patient is concerned . . ."

Conway muted the speaker which carried the conversation between ship and receptionist into the gallery and said, "This is as good a time as any to explain our physiological classification system to you. Briefly, that is, because later there will be special lectures on this subject."

Clearing his throat, he began, "In the four-letter classification system the first letter indicates the level of physical evolution, the second denotes the type and distribution of limbs and sense organs and the other two the combination metabolism and pressure and gravity requirements, which in turn give an indication of the physical mass and form of protective tegument possessed by the being. I must mention here, in case any of you might feel inferior regarding your classification, that the level of physical evolution has no relation to the level of intelligence . . ."

Species with the prefix A, B and C, he went on to explain, were water-breathers. On most worlds life had originated in the sea and these beings had developed high intelligence without having to leave it. D through F were warm-blooded oxygen-breathers, into which group fell most of the intelligence races in the galaxy, and the G and K types were also oxygen-breathing but insectile. The Ls and Ms were light-gravity, winged beings.

36

Chlorine-breathing life-forms were contained in the O and P groups, and after that came the more exotic, the more highly-evolved physically and the downright weird types. Radiation-eaters, frigid-blooded or crystalline beings, and entities capable of modifying their physical structure at will. Those possessing extra-sensory powers sufficiently well-developed to make walking or manipulatory appendages unnecessary were given the prefix V, regardless of size or shape.

Conway admitted to anomalies in the system, but these could be blamed on the lack of imagination by its originators. One of the species present in the observation gallery was a case in point—the AACP type with its vegetable metabolism. Normally the A prefix denoted a water-breather, there being nothing lower in the system than the piscatorial life-forms. But the AACPs were vegetables and plants had come before fish.

"... Great stress is laid on the importance of a rapid and accurate classification of incoming patients, who very often are in no condition to furnish this information themselves," Conway went on. "Ideally, you should reach a stage of proficiency which will enable you to rattle off a classification after a three-second glimpse of an e-t foot or section of tegument.

"But look there," he said, pointing.

Over the control desk three screens were alight, and adjacent indicators added detail to the information contained in the pictures. The first showed the interior of Lock Three, which contained two Earth-human orderlies and a large stretcher-carrier. The orderlies wore heavy duty suits and anti-gravity belts, which didn't surprise Conway at all because Lock Three and its associated levels were maintained at five Gs with pressure to match. Another screen showed the exterior of the lock with its transfer servo-mechanisms and the ship about to make contact, and the third picture was being relayed from inside the ship and showed the patient.

Conway said, "You can see that it is a heavy, squat life-form possessing six appendages which serve both as arms and legs. Its skin is thick, very tough and pitted all over, and is also incrusted in places with a dry, brownish substance which sometimes flakes off when the patient moves. Pay particular attention to this brown substance, and to features which seem to be missing from the body. The tell-tales show a warm-blooded, oxygen-breathing metabolism adapted to a gravity pull of four Gs. Would one of you like to classify it for me?"

There was a long silence, then the Creppelian AMSL twitched a tentacle and said, "FROL, sir."

"Very close," said Conway approvingly. "However, I happen to know that this being's atmosphere is a dense, nearly opaque soup, the resemblance to soup being increased by the fact that its lower reaches are alive with small airborne organisms which it feeds upon. You missed the fact that it has no eating mouth but absorbs food directly via the pittings in its skin. When travelling in space, however, the food has to be sprayed on, hence the brownish incrustation—"

"FROB," said the Creppelian quickly.

"Correct."

Conway wondered whether this AMSL was a little brighter than the others or just less shy. He made a mental note to keep an eye on this particular batch of trainees. He could use a bright assistant in his own wards.

Waving goodbye to the furry receptionist, Conway gathered his flock about him again and headed them towards the FGLI ward five levels below. After that came other wards until Conway decided to introduce them to the complex, far flung department of the Hospital without whose constant and efficient working the tremendous establishment of Sector General could not have functioned and the vast multitude of its patients, staff and maintenance personnel could not have lived.

Conway was feeling hungry, and it was time he showed them where they all ate.

AACPs did not eat in the normal manner but planted themselves during their sleep period in specially prepared soil and absorbed nutriment in that way. After seeing them settled he deposited the PVSJ in the dim, noisome depths of the hall where the chlorine-breathers ate, and this left him with the two DBLFs and the AMSL to dispose of.

The largest dining hall in the hospital, the one devoted to oxygen-breathers, was close by. Conway saw the two Kelgians placed with a group of their own species, then with a look of hungry yearning towards the Senior's enclosure he hurried out again to take care of the Creppelian.

To reach the section catering for the water-breathers necessitated a fifteen minute walk along some of the busiest corridors of the hospital. Entities of all shapes and sizes flapped, undulated and sometimes walked past them. Conway had become inured to being jostled by elephantine Tralthans and having to step carefully around the fragile, diminutive LSVOs, but the Creppelian was like an armour plated octopus walking on eggs—there were times when the AMSL seemed afraid to move. The bubbling sounds from its suit had increased noticably, too.

Conway tried to make it relax by getting it to talk about its previous hospital experience, but without much success. Then suddenly they turned a corner and Conway saw his old friend Prilicla coming from a side ward...

The AMSL went "Wheep!" and its eight legs threshed frantically into reverse. One of them swung heavily into the back of Conway's knees and he sat down violently. The octopoid took off down the corridor, still wheeping.

"What the blazes...!" said Conway, with what he thought later was commendable restraint.

"This is my fault entirely, I frightened it," said Prilicla as it hurried up. "Are you hurt, Doctor?"

"*You* frightened it...!"

The gentle, spider-like creature from Cinruss apologised, "Yes, I'm afraid so. The combination of surprise and what seems to be a deeply-rooted xenophobic neurosis caused a panic reaction. It is badly frightened but not completely out of control. Are you hurt, Doctor?"

"Just my feelings," Conway growled, scrambling to his feet and going after the fleeing Creppelian, who was now out of sight and very nearly out of earshot.

His progress in the wake of the AMSL became a rapid zigzag that was half sprint and half waltz. To his superiors he called "Excuse me!" and to equals and inferiors he bawled "Gangway!" Almost at once he began to overtake the AMSL, proving once again that as an efficient means of locomotion two feet were much better than eight, and he was just drawing level when the being trapped itself neatly by turning into a linen storeroom. Conway skidded to a halt outside the still open door, went in and closed it firmly behind him.

As calmly as shortage of breath would allow he said, "Why did you run away?"

Words poured suddenly from the AMSL. The Translator filtered out all the emotional overtones but from the sheer rapidity of its speech he knew that the Creppelian was having the equivalent of hysterics, and as he listened he knew that Prilicla's emotional reading had been right. Here was an xenophobic neurosis and no mistake.

*O'Mara will get you if you don't watch out,* he thought grimly.

Given even the highest qualities of tolerance and mutual respect, there were still occasions when inter-racial friction occurred in the hospital. Potentially dangerous situations arose through ignorance or misunderstanding, or a being could develop xenophobia to a degree which affected its professional efficiency, mental stability, or both. An Earth-human doctor, for instance, who had a subconscious fear of spiders would not be able to bring to bear on a Cinrusskin patient the proper degree of clinical detachment necessary for its treatment. And if one of the Cinrusskins, like Prilicla, were to treat such an Earth-human patient . . .

It was O'Mara's job as Chief Psychologist to detect and eradicate such trouble—or if all else failed, to remove the potentially dangerous individuals—before such friction developed into open conflict. Conway did not know how O'Mara would react to a hulking great AMSL who fled in panic from such a fragile creature as Dr. Prilicla.

When the Creppelian's outburst began to ease off Conway raised his hand for attention and said, "I realise now that Dr. Prilicla bears a physical resemblance to a species of small, amphibious predator native to your home world, and that in your youth you experienced an extremely harrowing incident with these animals. But Doctor Prilicla is not an animal and the resemblance is purely visual. Far from being a threat you could kill Prilicla if you were to touch it carelessly.

"Knowing this," Conway ended seriously, "would you be frightened into running if you were to meet this being again?"

"I don't know," said the AMSL. "I might."

Conway sighed. He could not help remembering his own first weeks at Sector General and the horrible, nightmare creatures which had haunted his sleep. What had made the nightmares particularly horrifying had been the fact that they were not figments of his imagination but actual, physical realities which in many cases were only a few bulkheads away.

He had never fled from any of these nightmares who had later become his teachers, colleagues and eventually friends. But to be honest with himself this was not due so much to intestinal fortitude as the fact that extreme fear had a tendency to paralyse Conway rather than to make him run away.

"I think you may need psychiatric assistance, Doctor," he told the Creppelian gently, "and the hospital's Chief Psychologist will help you. But I would advise you not to consult him at once. Spend a week or so trying to adapt to the situation before going to him. You will find that he will think more highly of you for doing this . . ."

. . . *And less likely*, he added silently, *to send you packing as unsuited for duty in a multi-environment hospital.*

The Creppelian left the storeroom with very little persuasion, after Conway told it that Prilicla was the only GLNO in the hospital at the moment and that their paths were very unlikely to cross twice in the same day. Ten minutes later the AMSL was settled in its dining tank and Conway was making for his own dinner by the fastest possible route.

# Chapter Seven

BY A stroke of luck he saw Dr. Mannen at an otherwise empty table in the Senior's enclosure. Mannen was an Earth-human who had once been Conway's superior and was now a Senior Physician well on the way to achieving Diagnostician status. Currently he was allowed to retain three physiology tapes—those of a Tralthan specialist in micro-surgery and two which had been made by surgeons of the low-gravity LSVO and MSVK species—but despite this his reactions were reasonably human. At the moment he was working through a salad with his eyes turned towards Heaven and the dining hall ceiling in an effort not to look at what he was eating. Conway sat down facing him and made a sympathetic, querying noise.

"I've had a Tralthan *and* a LSVO on my list this afternoon, both long jobs," Mannen said grumpily. "You know how it is, I've been thinking like them too much. If only these blasted Tralthans weren't vegetarians, or the LSVOs weren't sickened by anything which doesn't look like bird seed. Are you anybody else today?"

41

Conway shook his head. "Just me. Do you mind if I have steak?"

"No, just don't talk about it."

"I won't."

Conway knew only too well the confusion, mental double vision and the severe emotional disturbance which went with a physiology tape that had become too thoroughly keyed in to the operating physician's mind. He could remember a time only three months ago when he had fallen hopelessly—but *hopelessly*—in love with one of a group of visiting specialists from Melf IV. The Melfans were ELNTs—six-legged, amphibious, vaguely crab-like beings—and while one half of his mind had insisted that the whole affair was ridiculous the other half thought lovingly of that gorgeously marked carapace and generally felt like baying at the moon.

Physiology tapes were decidedly a mixed blessing, but their use was necessary because no single being could hope to hold in its brain all the physiological data needed for the treatment of patients in a multi-environment hospital. The incredible mass of data required to take care of them was furnished by means of Educator tapes, which were simply the brain recordings of great medical specialists of the various species concerned. If an Earth-human doctor had to treat a Kelgian patient he took one of the DBLF physiology tapes until treatment was complete, after which he had it erased. But Senior Physicians with teaching duties were often called on to retain these tapes for long periods, which wasn't much fun at all.

The only good thing from their point of view was that they were better off than the Diagnosticians.

They were the hospital's *elite*. A Diagnostician was one of those rare beings whose mind was considered stable enough to retain permanently up to ten physiology tapes simultaneously. To their data-crammed minds was given the job of original research in xenological medicine and the diagnosis and treatment of new diseases in hitherto unknown life-forms. There was a well-known saying in the hospital, reputed to have originated with O'Mara himself, that anyone sane enough to want to be a Diagnostician was mad.

For it was not only physiological data which the tapes imparted, the complete memory and personality of the entity who had possessed that knowledge was impressed on the receiving brain as well. In effect a Diagnostician subjected

42

himself or itself voluntarily to the most drastic form of multiple schizophrenia, with the alien personality sharing his mind so utterly *different* that in many cases they did not have even a system of logic in common.

Conway brought his thoughts back to the here and now. Mannen was speaking again.

"A funny thing about the taste of salad," he said, still glaring at the ceiling as he ate, "is that none of my alter egos seem to mind it. The sight of it yes, but not the taste. They don't particularly like it, mind, but neither does it completely revolt them. At the same time there are few species with an overwhelming passion for it, either. And speaking of overwhelming passions, how about you and Murchison?"

One of these days Conway expected to hear gears clashing, the way Mannen changed subjects so quickly.

"I'll be seeing her tonight if I've time," he replied carefully. "However, we're just good friends."

"Haw," said Mannen.

Conway make an equally violent switch of subjects by hurriedly breaking the news about his latest assignment. Mannen was the best in the world, but he had the painful habit of pulling a person's leg until it threatened to come off at the hip. Conway managed to keep the conversation off Murchison for the rest of the meal.

As soon as Mannen and himself split up he went to the intercom and had a few words with the doctors of various species who would be taking over the instruction of the trainees, then he looked at his watch. There was almost an hour before he was due aboard *Vespasian*. He began to walk a little more hurriedly than befitted a Senior Physician . . .

The sign over the entrance read "Recreation Level, Species DBDG, DBLF, ELNT, GKNM & FGLI." Conway went in, changed his whites for shorts and began searching for Murchison.

Trick lighting and some really inspired landscaping had given the recreation level the illusion of tremendous spaciousness. The overall effect was of a small, tropical beach enclosed on two sides by cliffs and open to the sea, which stretched out to a horizon rendered indistinct by heat haze. The sky was blue and cloudless—realistic cloud effects were difficult to reproduce, a maintenance engineer had told him—

and the water of the bay was deep blue shading to torquoise. It lapped against the golden, gently sloping beach whose sand was almost too warm for the feet. Only the artificial sun, which was too much on the reddish side for Conway's taste, and the alien greenery fringing the beach and cliff's kept it from looking like a tropical bay anywhere on Earth.

But then space was at a premium in Sector General and the people who worked together were expected to play together as well.

The most effective, yet completely unseen, aspect of the place was the fact that it was maintained at one-half normal gravity. A half-G meant that people who were tired could relax more comfortably and the ones who were feeling lively could feel livelier still, Conway thought wryly as a steep, slow-moving wave ran up the beach and broke around his knees. The turbulence in the bay was not produced artificially, but varied in proportion to the size, number and enthusiasm of the bathers using it.

Projecting from one of the cliffs were a series of diving ledges connected by concealed tunnels. Conway climbed to the highest, fifty-foot ledge and from this point of vantage tried to find a DBDG female in a white swimsuit called Murchison.

She wasn't in the restaurant on the other cliff, or in the shallows adjoining the beach, or in the deep green water under the diving ledges. The sand was thickly littered with reclining forms which were large, small, leathery, scaley and furry —but Conway had no difficulty separating the Earth-human DBDG's from the general mass, they being the only intelligent species in the Federation with a nudity taboo. So he knew that anyone wearing clothing, no matter how abbreviated, was what *he* considered a human being.

Suddenly he caught a glimpse of white which was partly obscured by two patches of green and one of yellow standing around it. That would be Murchison, all right. He took a quick bearing and retraced his steps.

When Conway approached the crowd around Murchison, two Corpsmen and an intern from the eighty-seventh level dispersed with obvious reluctance. In a voice which, much to his disgust, had gone up in pitch, he said, "Hi. Sorry I'm late."

Murchison shielded her eyes to look up at him. "I just arrived myself," she said, smiling. "Why don't you lie down?"

44

Conway dropped onto the sand but remained propped on one elbow, looking at her.

Murchison possessed a combination of physical features which made it impossible for any Earth-human male member of the staff to regard her with anything like clinical detachment, and regular exposure to the artificial but UV-rich sun had given her a deep tan made richer by the dazzling contrast of her white swimsuit. Dark auburn hair stirred restively in the artificial breeze, her eyes were closed again and her lips slightly parted. Her respiration was slow and deep, that of a person either perfectly relaxed or asleep, and the things it was doing to her swimsuit was also doing things to Conway. He thought suddenly that if she was telepathic at this moment she would be up and running for dear life . . .

"You look," she said, opening one eye, "like somebody who wants to growl deep in his throat and beat his manly, clean-shaven chest—"

"It isn't clean-shaven," Conway protested, "it's just naturally not hairy. But I want you to be serious for a moment. I'd like to talk to you, alone, I mean . . ."

"I don't care either way about chests," she said soothingly, "so you don't have to feel bad about it."

"I don't," said Conway, then doggedly; "Can't we get away from this menagerie and . . .Oops, stampede!"

He reached across quickly and clapped his hand over her eyes, simultaneously closing his own.

Two Tralthans on a total of twelve, elephantine feet thundered past within a few yards of them and ploughed into the shallows, scattering sand and spray over a radius of fifty yards. The half-G conditions which allowed the normally slow and ponderous FGLIs to gambol like lambs also kept the sand they had kicked up airborne for a considerable time. When Conway was sure that the last grains had settled he took his hand away from Murchison's eyes. But not completely.

Hesitantly, a little awkwardly, he slid his hand over the soft warm contour of her cheek until he was cupping the side of her jaw in his palm. Then gently he pushed his fingers into the soft tangle of curls behind her ear. He felt her stiffen, then relax again.

"Uh, see what I mean," he said dry-mouthed. "Unless you *like* half-ton bullies kicking sand in your face . . ."

45

"We'll be alone later," said Murchison, laughing, "when you take me home."

"And then what happens!" Conway said disgustedly. "Just the same as last time. We'll sneak up to your door, being very careful not to wake your room-mate who has to go on early duty, and then that damned servo will come trundling up . . ." Angrily, Conway began to mimic the taped voice of the robot as he went on, ". . . I perceive that you are beings of classification DBDG and are of differing genders, and note further that you have been in close juxtaposition for a period of two minutes forty-eight seconds. In the circumstances I must respectfully remind you of Regulation Twenty-one, sub-Section Three regarding the entertaining of visitors in DBDG Nurses Quarters . . ."

Almost choking, Murchison said, "I'm sorry, it must have been very frustrating for you."

Conway thought sourly that the expression of sorrow was rather spoiled by the suppressed laughter preceeding it. He leaned closer and took her gently by the shoulder. He said, "It was and is. I want to talk to you and I won't have time to see you home tonight. But I don't want to talk here, you always head for the water when I get you cornered. Well, I want to get you in a corner, both literally and conversationally, and ask some serious questions. This being friends is killing me . . ."

Murchison shook her head. She took his hand away from her shoulder, squeezed it and said, "Let's swim."

Seconds later as he chased her into the shallows he wondered if perhaps she wasn't a little telepathic after all. She was certainly running fast enough.

In half-G conditions swimming was an exhilarating experience. The waves were high and steep and the smallest splash seemed to hang in the air for seconds, with individual drops sparkling red and amber in the sun. A badly executed dive by one of the heavier life-forms—the FGLIs especially had an awful lot of belly to flop—could cause really spectacular effects. Conway was threshing madly after Murchison on the fringe of just such a titanic upheaval when a loudspeaker on the cliff roared into life.

"Doctor Conway," it boomed. "Will Doctor Conway report at Lock Sixteen for embarkation, please . . ."

They were walking rapidly up the beach when Murchison

said, very seriously for her, "I didn't know you were leaving. I'll change and see you off."

There was a Monitor Corps officer in the lock antechamber. When he saw Conway had company he said, "Doctor Conway? We leave in fifteen minutes, sir," and disappeared tactfully. Conway stopped beside the boarding tube and so did Murchison. She looked at him but there was no particular expression on her face, it was just beautiful and very desirable. Conway went on telling her about his important new assignment although he didn't want to talk about that at all. He talked rapidly and nervously until he heard the Monitor officer returning along the tube, then he pulled Murchison tightly against him and kissed her hard.

He couldn't tell if she responded. He had been too sudden, too ungentle ...

"I'll be gone about three months," he said, in a voice which tried to explain and apologise at the same time. Then with forced lightness he ended, "And in the morning I won't feel a bit sorry."

## Chapter Eight

CONWAY WAS shown to his cabin by an officer wearing a medic's caduceus over his insignia who introduced himself as Major Stillman. Although he spoke quietly and politely Conway got the impression that the Major was not a person who would be overawed by anything or anybody. He said that the Captain would be pleased to see Conway in the control room after they had made the first jump, to welcome him aboard personally.

A little later Conway met Colonel Williamson, the ship's Captain, who gave him the freedom of the ship. This was a courtesy rare enough on a government ship to impress Conway, but he soon discovered that although nobody said anything he was simply in everyone's way in the control room, and twice he lost himself while trying to explore the ship's interior. The Monitor heavy cruiser *Vespasian* was much larger than Conway had realised. After being guided back by a friendly Corpsman with a too-expressionless face he decided that he would spend most of the trip in his cabin familiarising himself with his new assignment.

Colonel Williamson had given him copies of the more detailed and recent information which had come in through Monitor Corps channels, but he began by studying the file which O'Mara had given him.

The being Lonvellin had been on the way to a world, about which it had heard some very nasty rumours, in a practically unexplored section of the Lesser Megellanic Cloud, when it had been taken ill and admitted to Sector General. Shortly after being pronounced cured it had resumed the journey and a few weeks later it had contacted the Monitor Corps. It had stated that conditions on the world it had found were both sociologially complex and medically barbaric, and that it would need advice on the medical side before it could begin to act effectively against the many social ills afflicting this truly distressed planet. It had also asked if some beings of physiological classification DBDG could be sent along to act as information gatherers as the natives were of that classification and were violently hostile to all off-planet life, a fact which seriously hampered Lonvellin's activities.

The fact of Lonvellin asking for help of any sort was surprising in itself in view of the enormous intelligence and experience of his species in solving vast sociological problems. But on this occasion things had gone disastrously wrong, and Lonvellin had been kept too busy using its defensive science to do anything else . . .

According to Lonvellin's report it had begun by observing the planet from space during many rotations, monitoring the radio transmissions through its Translator, and taking particular note of the low level of industrialisation which contrasted so oddly with the single, still functioning space port. When all the information which it had thought necessary had been collected and evaluated it chose what it considered to be the best place to land.

From the evidence at hand Lonvellin judged the world —the native's name for it was Etla—to have been a once-prosperous colony which had regressed for economic reasons until now it had very little contact with outside. But it did have some, which meant that Lonvellin's first and usually most difficult job, that of making the natives trust an alien

48

and perhaps visually horrifying being who had dropped out of the sky, was greatly simplified. These people would know about e-ts. So it took the role of a poor, frightened, slightly stupid extra-terrestrial who had been forced to land to make repairs to its ship. For this it would require various odd and completely worthless chunks of metal or rock, and it would pretend great difficulty in making the Etlans understand exactly what it needed. But for these valueless pieces of rubbish it could exchange items of great value, and soon the more enterprising natives would get to know about it.

At this stage Lonvellin expected to be exploited shamelessly, but it didn't mind. Gradually things would change. Rather than give items of value it would offer to perform even more valuable services. It would let it be known that it now considered its ship to be irrepairable, and gradually it would become accepted as a permanent resident. After that it would be just a matter of time, and time was something with which Lonvellin was particularly well supplied.

It landed close to a road which ran between two small towns, and soon had the chance to reveal itself to a native. The native, despite Lonvellin's careful contact and many reassurances via the Translator, fled. A few hours later small, crude projectiles with chemical warheads began falling on his ship and the whole area, which was densely wooded, had been saturated with volatile chemicals and deliberately set alight.

Lonvellin had been unable to proceed without knowing why this race with experience of space-travel should be so blindly hostile to e-ts, and not being in a position to ask questions himself it had called for Earth-human assistance. Shortly afterwards Alien Contact specialists of the Monitor Corps had arrived, sized up the situation for themselves and gone in.

Quiet openly, as it happened.

They discovered that the natives were terrified of e-ts because they believed them to be disease carriers. What was even more peculiar was the fact that they were not worried by off-planet visitors of their own species or a closely similar race, members of which would have been more likely to be carriers of disease: because it was a well-known medical fact that diseases which affected extra-terrestrials were not communicable to members of other planetary species. Any race with a knowledge of space travel should know *that*, Conway thought. It was the first thing a star-traveling culture learned.

He was trying to make some sense out of this strange contradiction, using a tired brain and some hefty reference works on the Federation's colonisation program, when Major Stillman's arrival made a very welcome interruption.

"We'll arrive in three days time, Doctor," the Major began, "and I think it's time you had some cloak and dagger training. By that I mean getting to know how to wear Etlan clothes. It's a very fetching costume, although personally I don't have the knees for a kilt..."

Etla had been contacted on two levels by the Corps, Stillman went on to explain. On one they had landed secretly using the native language and dress, no other disguise being necessary because the physiological resemblance had been so close. Most of their later information had been gained in this way and so far none of the agents had been caught. On the other level the Corpsmen admitted their extra-terrestrial origin, conversed by Translator, and their story was that they had heard of the plight of the native population and had come to give medical assistance. The Etlans had accepted this story, revealing the fact that similar offers of help had been made in the past, that an Empire ship was sent every ten years loaded with the newest drugs, but dispite all this the medical situation continued to worsen. The Corpsmen were welcome to try to relieve the situation if they could, but the impression given by the Etlans was that they were just another party of well-intentional bunglers.

Naturally when the subject of Lonvellin's landing came up the Corps had to pretend complete ignorance, and their expressed opinions leaned heavily toward the middle of the road.

It was a very complex problem, Stillman told him, and became more so with every new report sent in by undercover agents. But Lonvellin had a beautifully simple plan for clearing up the whole mess. When Conway heard it he wished suddenly that he hadn't tried to impress Lonvellin with his skill as a doctor. He would much rather have been back in the hospital right now. This being made responsible for organising the cure of an entire planetary population gave him an unpleasantly gone feeling in the region of his transverse colon...

Etla was beset with much sickness and suffering and

50

narrow, superstitious thinking, their reaction to Lonvellin being a shocking illustration of their intolerance towards species which did not resemble themselves. The first two conditions increased the third, which in turn worsened the first two. Lonvellin hoped to break this vicious circle by causing a marked improvement in the health of the population, one that would be apparent to even the least intelligent and big-oted natives. It would then have the Corpsmen admit publicly that they had been acting under Lonvellin's instruc-tions all along, which should make the e-t hating natives feel somewhat ashamed of themselves. Then during the perhaps temporary increase of e-t tolerance which would follow, Lon-vellin would set about gaining their trust and eventually re-turn to its original long-term plan for making them a sane, happy and thriving culture again.

Conway told Stillman that he wasn't an expert in these matters but it sounded like a very good plan.

Stillman said, "I am, and it is. If it works."

On the day before they were due to arrive the Captain asked if Conway would like to come to Control for a few minutes. They were computing their position in preparation for making the final jump and the ship had emerged relative-ly close to a binary system, one star of which was a short-term variable.

Awed, Conway thought it was the sort of spectacle which makes people feel small and alone, makes them feel the urge to huddle together and the need to talk so that they might re-establish their puny identities amid all the magnificence. Conversational barriers were down and all at once Captain Williamson was speaking in tones which suggested three things to the listening Conway—that the Captain might be human after all, that he had hair and that he was about to let it down a little.

"Er, Doctor Conway," he began apologetically, "I don't want to sound as if I'm criticising Lonvellin. Especially as it was a patient of yours and may also have been a friend. Neither do I want you to think that I'm annoyed because it has a Federation cruiser and various lesser units run-ning errands for it. That isn't so ..."

Williamson took off his cap and smoothed a wrinkle from the head-band with his thumb. Conway had a glimpse of thin-ning grey hair and a forehead whose deep worry lines had been concealed by the cap's visor. The cap was replaced and he became the calm, efficient senior officer again.

"... To put it bluntly, Doctor," he went on, "Lonvellin is what I would call a gifted amateur. Such people always seem to stir up trouble for us professionals, upsetting schedules and so on. But this doesn't bother me either, because the situation Lonvellin uncovered here most definitely needs something done about it. The point I'm trying to make is that, as well as our survey, colonisation and enforcement duties, we have experience at sorting out just such sociological tangles as this one, although at the same time I admit that there is no individual within the Corps with anything like Lonvellin's ability. Nor can we suggest any plan at the moment better than the one put forward by Lonvellin..."

Conway began to wonder if the Captain was getting at something or merely blowing off steam. Williamson had not struck him as being the complaining type.

"... As the person with most responsibility next to Lonvellin on this project," the Captain finished with a rush, "it is only fair that you know what we think as well as what we are doing. There are nearly twice as many of our people working on Etla than Lonvellin knows about, and more are on the way. Personally I have the greatest respect for our long-lived friend, but I can't help feeling that the situation here is more complex than even Lonvellin realises."

Conway was silent for a moment, then he said, "I've wondered why a ship like *Vespasian* was being used on what is basically a cultural study project. Do you think that the situation is more, ah, dangerous as well?"

"Yes," said the Captain.

At that moment the tremendous double-star system pictured in the view-screen dissolved and was replaced by that of a normal G-type sun and, within a distance of ten million miles, the tiny sickle shape of the planet which was their destination. Before Conway could put any of the questions he was suddenly itching to ask, the Captain informed him that they had completed their final jump, that from now until touchdown he would be a very busy man, and ended by politely throwing him out of the control room with the advice that he should catch as much sleep as possible before landing.

Back in his cabin Conway undressed thoughtfully and, a part of his mind was pleased to note, almost automatically.

Both Stillman and he had been wearing Etlan costume—blouse, kilt and a waist-sash with pockets, a beret and a dramatic calf-length cloak being added for outdoor use—continually for the past few days, so that now he felt comfortable in it even while dining with *Vespasian's* officers. At the moment, however, his discomfort was caused solely by the Captain's concluding remarks to him in the control room.

Williamson thought that the Etlan situation was dangerous enough to warrant using the largest type of law enforcement vessel possessed by the Monitor Corps. Why? Where was the danger?

Certainly there was nothing resembling a military threat on Etla. The very worst that the Etlans could do they had done to Lonvellin's ship and that had hurt the being's feelings and nothing else. Which meant that the danger had to come from somewhere outside.

Suddenly Conway thought he knew what was worrying the Captain. *The Empire* ...

Several of the reports had contained references to the Empire. It was the great unknown quantity so far. The Monitor Corps survey vessels had not made contact with it, which wasn't surprising because this sector of the galaxy was not scheduled for mapping for another fifty years, and would not have been entered if Lonvellin's project had not come unstuck. All that was known about the Empire was that Etla was part of it and that it sent medical aid at regular if lengthy intervals.

To Conway's mind the quality of that aid and the intervals between its arrival told an awful lot about the people responsible for sending it. They could not be medically advanced, he reasoned, or the drugs they sent would have checked, if only temporarily, some of the epidemics which had been sweeping Etla at the time. And they were almost certainly poor or the ships would have come at shorter intervals. Conway would not be surprised if the mysterious Empire turned out to be a mother world and a few struggling colonies like Etla. But most important of all, an Empire which regularly sent aid to its distressed colony, whether it was large, medium or small as Empires went, did not seem to Conway to be a particularly evil or dangerous entity. To the contrary, on the evidence available he rather approved of this Empire.

Captain Williamson, he thought as he rolled into bed, was inclined to worry too much.

## Chapter Nine

VESPASIAN LANDED. On the main screen in the Communications room Conway saw a cracked white expanse of concrete which stretched to the half-mile distant periphery, where the fine details of vegetation and architecture which would have made the scene alien were lost in the heat haze. Dust and dried leaves littered the concrete and small heaps of cloud were scattered untidily about a very Earth-like sky. The only other ship on the field was a Monitor courier vessel which was grounded close to the block of disused offices that had been loaned by the Etlan authorities for use as the visitor's surface base.

Behind Conway the Captain said, "You understand, Doctor, that Lonvellin is unable to leave its ship, and that any physical contact between us at this stage would wreck our present good relations with the natives. But this is a big screen. Excuse me . . ."

There was a click and Conway was looking into the control room of Lonvellin's ship, with a life-size image of Lonvellin itself sprawling across most of the picture.

"Greetings, friend Conway," the EPLH's voice boomed from the speaker. "It is a great pleasure to see you again."

"A pleasure to be here, sir," Conway replied, "I trust you are in good health . . .?"

The enquiry was not merely a polite formality. Conway wanted to know if there had been any more 'misunderstandings' on the cellular level between Lonvellin and its personal physician, the intelligent, organised virus-colony which dwelt within its patient-host's body. Lonvellin's doctor had caused quite a stir at Sector General, where they were still arguing as to whether it should be classified as a doctor or a disease . . .

"My health is excellent, Doctor," Lonvellin replied, then straightaway got down to the business in hand. Conway hastily returned his mind to present time and concentrated on what the EPLH was saying.

Conway's own instructions were general. He was to coordinate the work of data-gathering Corps medical officers on Etla and, because the sociological and medical aspects of the problem were so closely connected, he was advised to keep abreast of the developments outside his specialty. With the arrival of the latest reports the sociological problem seemed more confusing, and it was Lonvellin's hope that a mind trained for the complexities of a multi-environment hospital would be able to establish a sensible pattern among this welter of contradictory facts. Dr. Conway would no doubt appreciate the urgency of the matter, and wish to begin work immediately ...

"... And I would like data on the Earth-human Clarke who is operating in District Thirty-five," Lonvellin went on without a pause, "so that I may properly evaluate the reports of this being ..."

As Captain Williamson was giving the required information Stillman tapped Conway's arm and nodded for them to leave. Twenty minutes later they were in the back of a covered truck on the way to the perimeter. Conway's head and one ear had been swathed in bandages, and he felt anxious and a little stupid.

"We'll stay hidden until we're clear of the port," Stillman said reassuringly, "then we'll sit with the driver. Lots of Etlans travel with our people these days, but it might arouse suspicion for us to be seen coming from the ship. And we'll head straight for town instead of calling at ground headquarters. I think you should see some of your patients as soon as possible."

Seriously, Conway said, "I know the symptoms are purely psychosomatic, but both my feet seem to be in an advanced stage of frost-bite ..."

Stillman laughed. "Don't worry, Doctor," he said. "The translator bandaged to your ear will let you know everything that goes on, and you won't have to speak because I'll explain that your head injury has temporarily affected your speech centres. Later, however, when you begin to pick up a little of the language a good tip is to develop a stutter. An impediment of this kind disguises the fact that the sufferer does not have the local idiom or accent, the large fault concealing all the smaller ones.

"Not all our undercover people have advanced linguistic training," he added, "and such ruses are necessary. But the main thing to remember is not to stay in any one place long enough for the more definite oddities of behavior to be noticed ..."

At that point the driver remarked that they were coming level with a blonde whom he could cheerfully stay near for the rest of his life. Stillman went on, "Despite the coarse suggestions of Corpsman Briggs here, perhaps our best protection lies in our mental approach to the work, to the fact that our intentions towards these people are completely honorable. If we were hostile agents intent on sabotage, or gathering intelligence for a future act of war, we would be much more likely to be caught. We should be tensed up, trying too hard to be natural, too suspicious and are more inclined to make mistakes because of this."

Conway said drily, "You make it sound too easy." But he felt reassured nevertheless.

The truck left them in the centre of town and they began to walk around. The first thing Conway noticed was that there were very few large or new-looking buildings, but that even the oldest were very well kept, and that the Etlans had a very attractive way of decorating the outside of their houses with flowers. He saw the people, the men and women working, shopping or going about businesses which at the present moment he could not even guess at. He *had* to think of them as men and women, as being he and she rather than a collection of coldly alien its.

He saw the twisted limbs, the crutches, the disease scarred faces, his analytical eye detecting and isolating conditions which had been stamped out among the Federation citizenship over a century ago. And everywhere he saw a sight familiar to anyone who had ever been to or worked in a hospital, that of the less sick patient freely and unselfishly giving all the aid possible to those who were worse off than himself.

The sudden realisation that he was not in a hospital ward where such sights were pleasantly normal but in a city street brought Conway physically and mentally to a halt.

"What gets me," he said when he could speak again, "is that so many of these conditions are curable. Maybe all of them. We haven't had epilepsy for one hundred and fifty years ..."

"And you feel like running amuck with a hypo," Stillman put in grimly, "injecting all and sundry with the indicated specifics. But you have to remember that the whole planet is like this, and that curing a few would not help at all. You are in charge of a very big ward, Doctor."

"I've read the reports," Conway said shortly. "It's just that the printed figures did not prepare me for the actuality..."

He stopped with the sentence incomplete. They had paused at a busy intersection and Conway noticed that both pedestrian and vehicular traffic had either slowed or come to a halt. Then he saw the reason.

There was a large wagon coming along the street. Painted and draped completely in red it was, unlike the other vehicle around it, unpowered. Short handles projected at intervals along each side and at every handle an Etlan walked or limped or hobbled, pushing it along. Even before Stillman took his beret off and Conway followed suit he knew that he was seeing a funeral.

"We'll visit the local hospital now," Stillman said when it had gone past. "If asked, my story is that we are looking for a sick relative called Mennomer who was admitted last week. On Etla that is a name like Smith. But we're not likely to be questioned, because practically everybody does a stint of hospital work and the staff are used to the part-time help coming and going all the time. And should we run into a Corps medical officer, as well we might, don't recognise him.

"And in case you're worried about your Etlan colleagues wanting to look under your bandages," Stillman went on practically reading Conway's mind, "they are far too busy to be curious about injuries which have already been treated..."

They spent two hours in the hospital without once having to tell their story about the ailing Mennomer. It was obvious from the start that Stillman knew his way about the place, that he had probably worked there. But there were always too many Etlans about for Conway to ask if it had been as a Corpsman observer or an undercover part-time nurse. Once he caught a glimpse of a Corpsman medic watching an Etlan doctor draining a pleural cavity of its empyema, his expression showing how dearly he would have liked to roll up his dark green sleeves and wade in himself.

The surgeons wore bright yellow instead of white, some of the operative techniques verged on the barbaric and the concept of isolation wards or barrier nursing had never occurred to them—or perhaps it had occurred to them, Conway thought in an effort to be fair, but the utterly fantastic degree of overcrowding made it impracticable. Considering the facilities at their disposal and the gigantic problem it had to face, this was a very good hospital. Conway approved of it and, judging from what he had seen of its staff, he approved of them, too.

"These are nice people," Conway said rather inadequately at one point. "I can't understand them jumping Lonvellin the way they did, somehow they don't seem to be the type."

"But they did it," Stillman replied grimly. "Anything which hasn't two eyes, two ears, two arms and two legs, or which has these things but happens to have them in the wrong places, gets jumped. It's something drummed into them at a very early age, with their ABCs, practically. I wish we knew why."

Conway was silent. He was thinking that the reason he had been sent here was to organise medical aid for this planet, and that wandering in fancy dress over one small piece of the jigsaw was not going to solve the big puzzle. It was time he got down to some serious work.

As if reading Conway's mind again Stillman said, "I think we should go back now. Would you prefer to work in the office block or the ship, Doctor?"

Stillman, Conway thought, was going to be a very good *aide*. Aloud he said, "The office block, please. I get lost too easily in the ship."

And so Conway was installed in a small office with a large desk, a button for calling Stillman and some other less-vital communications equipment. After his first lunch in the officers dining quarters he ate all his meals in the office with Stillman. Sometimes he slept in the office and sometimes he didn't sleep at all. The days passed and his eyes began to feel like hot, gritty marbles in his head from reading reports and more reports. Stillman always kept them coming. Conway reorganised the medical investigation, bringing in some of the Corps doctors for discussion or flying out to those who could not for various reasons get in.

A large number of the reports were outside his province, being copies of information sent in by Williamson's men on purely sociological problems. He read them on the off-chance of their having a bearing on his own problem, which

58

many of them did, But they usually added to his puzzlement.

Blood samples, biopsys, specimens of all kinds began to flow in. They were immediately loaded onto a courier—the Corps had put three of them at his disposal now—and rushed to the Diagnostician-in-Charge of Pathology at Sector General. The results were sub-radioed back to *Vespasian*, taped, and the reels dumped on Conway's desk within a few days. The ship's main computor, or rather the section of it which wasn't engaged on Translator relay, was also placed at his disposal, and gradually the vaguest suggestion of a pattern seemed to be emerging out of the flood of related and unrelated facts. But it was a pattern which made no sense to anyone, least of all Conway. He was nearing the end of his fifth week on Etla and there was still very little progress to report to Lonvellin.

But Lonvellin wasn't pushing for results. It was a very patient being who had all the time in the world. Sometimes Conway found himself wondering if Murchison would be as patient as Lonvellin.


## *Chapter Ten*

IN ANSWER to his buzz Major Stillman, red-eyed and with his usually crisp uniform just slightly rumpled, stumbled in and sat down. They exchanged yawns, then Conway spoke.

"In a few days I'll have the supply and distribution figures needed to begin curing this place," he said. "Every serious disease has been listed together with information on the age, sex and geographical location of the patient, and the quantities of medication calculated. But before I give the go ahead for flooding the place with medical supplies I'd feel a lot easier in my mind if we knew exactly how this situation came about in the first place.

"Frankly, I'm worried," he went on. "I think we may be guilty of replacing the broken crockery while the bull is still loose in the china shop."

Stillman nodded, whether in agreement or with weariness Conway couldn't say.

On a planet which was an absolute pest-hole why were infant mortality figures, or deaths arising from complications or infections during childbirth so low? Why was there a marked tendency for infants to be healthy and the adults chronically ill? Admittedly a large proportion of the infant population were born blind or were physically impaired by inherited diseases, but relatively few of them died young. They carried their deformities and disfigurements through to late middle age where, statistically, most of them succumbed.

And there was also statistical evidence that the Etlans were guilty of gross exhibitionism in the matter of their diseases. They ran heavily to unpleasant skin conditions, maladies which caused gradual wasting or deformity of the limbs, and some pretty horrible combinations of both. And their costume did nothing to conceal their afflictions. To the contrary, Conway had the feeling sometimes that they were like so many small boys showing off their sore knees to their friends . . .

Conway realised that he had been thinking aloud when Stillman interrupted him suddenly.

"You're wrong, Doctor!" he said, sharply for him. "These people aren't masochists. Whatever went wrong here originally, they've been trying to fight it. They've been fighting, with very little assistance, for over a century and losing all the time. It surprises me they have a civilisation left at all. And they wear an abbreviated costume because they believe fresh air and sunlight is good for what ails them, and in most cases they are quite right.

"This belief is drilled into them from an early age," Stillman went on, his tone gradually losing its sharpness, "like their hatred of e-ts and the belief that isolating infectious diseases is unnecessary. Is dangerous, in fact, because they believe that the germs of one disease fight the germs of another so that both are weakened . . ."

Stillman shuddered at the thought and fell silent.

"I didn't mean to belittle our patients, Major," Conway said. "I have no sensible answers to this thing so my mind is throwing up stupid ones. But you mentioned the lack of assistance which the Etlans receive from their Empire. I would like more details on that, especially on how it is distributed. Better still, I'd like to ask the Imperial Representative on Etla about it. Have you been able to find him yet?"

Stillman shook his head and said drily, "This aid doesn't come like a batch of food parcels. There are drugs, of course, but most of it would be in the form of the latest medical literature relevent to the conditions here. How it reaches the people is something we are just now finding out ..."

Every ten years an Empire ship would land and be met by the Imperial Representative, Stillman went on to explain, and after unloading and handing over what were presumably dispatches it left again within a matter of hours. Apparently no citizen of the Empire would stay on Etla for a second longer than was necessary, which was understandable. Then the Imperial Representative, a personage called Teltrenn, set about distributing the medical aid.

But instead of using the mass distribution media to bring local medical authorities up to date on these new methods, and allow local GPs time to familiarise themselves with the theory and procedures before the medication arrived, Teltrenn sat tight on all the information until such times as he could pay them a personal visit. Then he handed everything over as being a personal gift from their glorious Emperor, accruing no small measure of glory himself by being the middleman, and the data which could have been in the hands of every doctor on the planet within three months reached them piecemeal in anything up to six years ...

"Six *years!*" said Conway, startled.

"Teltrenn isn't, so far as we've been able to find out, a very energetic person," Stillman said. "What makes matters worse is that little or no original medical research is being done on Etla, due to the absence of the researcher's most vital tool, the microscope. Etla can't make precision optical equipment and apparently no Empire ship has thought to bring them.

"It all boils down to the fact," Stillman ended grimly, "that the Empire does all of Etla's medical thinking for her, and the evidence suggests that medically the Empire is not very smart."

Conway said firmly, "I'd like to see the correlation between the arrival of this aid and the incidence of disease immediately thereafter. Can you help me in that?"

"There's a report just in which might help you," Stillman

replied. "It's a copy of the records of a North Continent hospital which go back past Teltrenn's last visit to them. The records show that he brought on that occasion some useful data on obstetrics and a specific against what we have called B-Eighteen. The incidence of B-Eighteen dropped rapidly within a few weeks there, although the overall figures remained much the same because F-Twenty-one began to appear about that time . . ."

B-Eighteen was analogous to a severe influenza, fatal to children and young adults in four cases out of ten. F-Twenty-one was a mild, non-fatal fever which lasted three to four weeks during which large, crescentric weals appeared all over the face, limbs and body. When the fever abated the weals darkened to a livid purple and remained for the rest of the patient's life.

Conway shook his head angrily. He said, "One of the main things wrong with Etla is its Imperial Representative!"

Standing up, Stillman said, "We want to ask him a few questions, too. We've advertised that fact widely by radio and print, so much so that we are now fairly certain that Teltrenn is hiding from us deliberately. Probably the reason is a guilty conscience over his mismanagement of affairs here. But a psych report, based on what hearsay evidence we have been able to gather about him, has been prepared for Lonvellin. I'll have them send a copy from the ship."

"Thank you," said Conway.

Stillman nodded, yawned and left. Conway thumbed his communicator switch, contacted *Vespasian* and asked for an audio link with the fifty miles distant Lonvellin. He was still worried and wanted to get it off his chest, the only trouble being he did not know exactly what 'it' was.

". . . You have done very well, friend Conway," Lonvellin said when he had finished speaking, "in fulfilling your part of the project so quickly, and I am fortunate indeed in the quality and eagerness of my assistants. We have now gained the trust of the Etlan doctors in most areas and the way will shortly be open to begin full-scale instruction in your latest curative techniques. You will therefore be returning to your hospital within a few days, and I urge that you do not leave with the feeling that you have not performed your assigned task in a completely satisfactory manner. These anxieties you mention are groundless.

"Your suggestion that the being Teltrenn should be removed

or replaced as part of the re-education program is sound," Lonvellin continued ponderously, "and I already had this step in mind. An added reason for removing it from office being the well-documented fact that it is the being largely responsible for keeping alive the widespread intolerance of off-planet life-forms. Your other suggestion that these harmful ideas may originate, not with Teltrenn but in the Empire, may or may not be correct. This does not, however, call for an immediate search for and investigation of the Empire which you urge."

Lonvellin's Translated voice was slow and necessarily emotionless, but Conway seemed to detect a hardening in its tone as it went on, "I perceive Etla as an isolated world kept in quarantine. The problem can therefore be solved without bringing in considerations of Empire influences or understanding fully the various inconsistencies which puzzle us both. These will become plain after its cure has been effected, and the answers we seek are of secondary importance to the planet-wide relief of suffering.

"Your contention that the visits of the Imperial ship," it went on, "which occur every ten years and last only a few hours, is a major factor in this problem is invalid. I might even suggest that, unconsciously perhaps, you are laying too much stress on this point merely that your curiosity regarding this Empire might be satisfied."

*You're so right*, Conway thought. But before he could reply the EPLH went on, "I wish to treat Etla as an isolated problem. Bringing in the Empire, which itself may or may not be in need of medical aid also, would enlarge the scope of the operation beyond managable limits.

"However, and purely to remove your evident anxiety," Lonvellin ended, "you may tell the being Williamson that it has my permission to scout for this Empire and report on conditions within it. In the event of it being found, however, no mention of what we are doing here on Etla is to be made until the operation is completed."

"I understand, sir," Conway said, and broke the connection. He thought it decidedly odd that Lonvellin had pinned his ears back for being curious, then almost with the same breath given him permission to indulge that curiosity. Was Lonvellin more concerned about the Empire's influence here than it cared to admit, or was the big beastie just going soft in its old age?

63

He called Captain Williamson.

The Captain hemmed a coupled of times when Conway had finished speaking and there was a distinctly embarrassed note in his voice when he replied. He said, "We've had a number of officers, both medical and cultural contact people, searching for the Empire for the last two months, Doctor. One of them has been successful and sent in a preliminary report. It comes from a medical officer who was not attached to the Etla project, and knows very little of what has been happening here, so it may not be as informative as you might wish. I'll send you a copy with the material on Teltrenn."

Coughing slightly, Williamson ended, "Lonvellin will have to be informed of this, naturally, but I must leave it to your discretion *when* you tell it."

Suddenly Conway laughed out loud. "Don't worry, Colonel, I'll sit on the information for a while. But if you *are* found out you can always remind Lonvellin that the function of a good servant is to anticipate the wishes of his master."

He continued laughing softly after Williamson signed off, then all at once the reaction set in.

Conway hadn't laughed much since coming to Etla. And he had not been guilty of over-identifying with his patients—no half-way decent doctor with the good of his charges at heart would commit that crime. It was just that nobody laughed very much on Etla. There was something in the atmosphere of the place, a feeling comprised both of urgency and hopelessness which seemed to intensify with each day that passed. It was rather like the atmosphere in a ward where a patient was going to die, Conway thought, except that even in those circumstances people found time to make cracks and relax for a few minutes between crises ...

Conway was beginning to miss Sector General. He was glad that in a few days he would be going back, despite his feeling of dissatisfaction over all the loose ends he was leaving untied. He began to think about Murchison.

That was something he had not done very often on Etla, either. Twice he had sent messages to her with the Elan specimens. He knew that Thornnastor in Pathology would see that she got them, even though Thornnastor was an FGLI with only the barest of passing interests in the emotional involvements of Earth-human DBDGs. But Murchison was the undemonstrative type. She might consider that going to the trouble of smuggling back a reply would be giving him too much encouragement, or maybe that kiss and run episode at the airlock had soured her on him completely. She was a peculiar girl. Very serious-minded, extremely dedicated, absolutely no time for men.

The first time she agreed to date him it had been because Conway had just pulled off a slick op and wanted to celebrate, and that previously he had worked with her on a case without once making a pass. Since then he had dated Murchison regularly and had been the envy of all the male DBDGs in the hospital. The only trouble was that they had nothing to be envious about . . .

His lugubrious train of thought was interrupted by the arrival of a Corpsman who dropped a folder onto his desk and said, "The material on Teltrenn, Doctor. The other report was confidential to Colonel Williamson and has to be copied by his Writer. We'll have it for you in fifteen minutes."

"Thank you," said Conway. The Corpsman left and he began to read.

Being a colony world which had not had the chance to grow naturally, Etla did not have national boundaries or the armed forces which went with them, but the police force enforcing the law on the planet were technically soldiers of the Emperor and under the command of Teltrenn. It had been a force of these policemen-soldiers who had attacked, and were still attacking, Lonvellin's ship. At first appraisal, the report stated, the evidence pointed to Teltrenn having a personality which was proud and power-hungry, but the cruelty usually found in such personalities was absent. In his relations with the native population—the Imperial Representative had not been born on Etla—Teltrenn showed fairness and consideration. It was plain that he looked down on the natives—'way down, almost as if they were members of a lower species. But he did not, openly, despise them, and he was never cruel to them.

Conway threw down the report; this was another stupid piece of an already senseless puzzle, and all at once he was sick of the whole silly business. He rose and stamped into the outer office, sending the door crashing against the wall. Stillman twitched slightly and looked up.

"Dump that paperwork until morning!" Conway snapped. "Tonight we are going to indulge shamelessly in pleasures of the flesh. We're going to sleep in our own cabins . . ."

"Sleep?" said Stillman, grinning suddenly. "What's that?"

"I don't know," said Conway, "I thought you might. I hear it's a new sensation, unutterable bliss and very habit-forming. Shall we live dangerously . . . ?"

"After you," said Stillman.

Outside the office block the night was pleasantly cool. There was broken cloud on the horizon but above them the stars seemed to crowd down, bright and thick and cold. This was a dense region of space, a fact further proved by the meteorites which made white scratches across the sky every few minutes. Altogether it was an inspiring and calming sight, but Conway could not stop worrying. He was convinced that he was missing something, and his anxiety was much worse out here under the sky than it had been at any time in the office. Suddenly he wanted to read that report on the Empire as quickly as possible.

To Stillman, he said, "Do you ever think of something, then feel horribly ashamed for having the kind of dirty mind which thinks thoughts like that?"

Stillman grunted, treating it as a rhetorical question, and they continued walking towards the ship. Abruptly they stopped.

On the Southern horizon the sun seemed to be rising. The sky had become a pale, rich blue which shaded through tor-quoise into black, and the bases of the distant clouds burned pink and gold. Then before they could appreciate, or even react to this glorious, misplaced sunrise it had faded to an angry red smudge on the horizon. They felt a tiny shock transmitted through the soles of their shoes, and a little later they heard a noise like distant thunder.

"Lonvellin's ship!" said Stillman.

They began to run.

# Chapter Eleven

THE COMMUNICATIONS room on *Vespasian* was a whirlwind of activity with the Captain forming its calm and purposeful centre. When Stillman and Conway arrived orders had gone out to the courier ship and all available helicopters to load decontamination and rescue gear and proceed to the blast area to render all possible aid. There was, of course, no hope for the Etlan force which had been surrounding Lonvellin's ship, but there were isolated farms and at least one small village on the fringe area. The rescuers would have to deal with panic as well as radiation casualties, because the Etlans had no experience of nuclear explosions and would almost certainly resist evacuation.

Out on the field, when Conway had seen Lonvellin's ship go up and had realised what it meant, he had felt physically ill. And now, listening to Williamson's urgent but unhurried orders going out, he felt cold sweat trickle down his forehead and spine. He licked his lips and said, "Captain, I have an urgent suggestion to make..."

He did not speak loudly, but there was something in his tone which made Williamson swing round immediately.

"This accident to Lonvellin means that you are in charge of the project, Doctor," Williamson said impatiently. "There is no need for such diffidence."

"In that case," said Conway in the same low, tense voice, "I have orders for you. Call off the rescue attempts and order everyone back to the ship. Take off before we are bombed, too..."

Conway saw them all looking at him, at his white, sweating face and frightened eyes, and he could see them all jumping to wrong conclusions. Williamson looked angry, embarrassed and completely at a loss for a few seconds, then his expression hardened. He turned to an officer beside him, snapped an order, then swung to face Conway again.

"Doctor," he began stiffly, "I have just put out our secondary meteor shield. Any solid object greater than one inch in diameter approaching from any direction whatever will be detected at a distance of one hundred miles and automatically deflected by pressors. So I can assure you, Doctor, that we are in no danger from any hypothetical attack with atomic missiles. The idea of a nuclear bombardment here is ridiculous, anyway. There is no atomic power on Etla, none whatever. We have instruments... You must have read the report.

"My *suggestion*," the Captain went on, in exactly the tone he used to suggest that the junior astrogator make an alteration in course, "is that we rush all possible help to the sur-

67

vivors of the blow-up, which must have been caused by a fault in Lonvellin's power pile..."

"Lonvellin wouldn't have a faulty pile!" Conway said harshly. "Like many long-lived beings it suffered from a constant and increasing fear of death the longer its life went on. It had the ultimate in personal physicians so that illness would not shorten its already tremendous life-span, and it follows that it would not have endangered itself by using a ship which was anything but mechanically perfect.

"Lonvellin was killed," Conway went on grimly, "and the reason they hit its ship first is probably because they dislike e-ts so much. And it's nice to know that you can protect the ship, but if we leave now they might not launch another missile at all, and our people out there and a lot more Etlans would not have to die..."

It was no good, Conway thought sickly. Williamson looked angry and embarrassed and stubborn—angry at being given apparently senseless orders, embarrassed because it looked as though Conway was behaving like a frightened old woman and stubborn because he thought he and not Conway was right. *Get the lead out of your pants, you unprintable fool!* Conway raged at him, but under his breath. He could not address such words to a Monitor Colonel surrounded by junior officers, and for the added reason that Williamson was not nor ever had been a fool. He was a reasonable, intelligent, highly competent officer. It was just that he had not had the chance to put the facts together properly. He didn't have any medical training, nor did he have a nasty, suspicious mind like Conway...

"You have a report on the Empire for me," he said instead. "Can I read it?"

Williamson's eyes flickered towards the battery of viewscreens surrounding them. All showed scenes of frantic activity—a helicopter being readied for flight, another staggering off the ground with a load obviously in excess of the safety limit, and a stream of men and decontamination equipment being rushed through the lock of the courier ship. He said, "You want to read it *now* ... ?"

"Yes," said Conway, then quickly shook his head as another idea struck him. He had been trying desperately to make Williamson take off immediately and leave the explanations until later when there was time to give them, but it was obvious now that he would have to explain first, and fast. He said, "I've a theory which explains what has been going on here and the report should verify it. But if I can tell you what I think is in that report before reading it, will you give my theory enough credence to do what I tell you and take off at once?"

Outside the ship both 'copters were climbing into the night sky, the courier boat was sealing her lock and a collection of surface transport, both Etlan and Monitor, was dispersing towards the perimeter. More than half of the ship's crew were out there, Conway knew, together with all the land-based Corpsmen who could possibly be spared—all heading for the scene of the blow-up and all piling up the distance between themselves and *Vespasian* with every second which passed.

Without waiting for Williamson's reply, Conway rushed on, "My guess is that it is an Empire in the strict sense of the word, not a loose Federation like ours. This means an extensive military organisation to hold it together and implement the laws of its Emperor, and the government on individual worlds would also be an essentially military one. All the citizens would be DBDGs like the Etlans and ourselves, and on the whole pretty average people except for their antipathy towards extra-terrestrials, who they have had little opportunity of getting to know so far."

Conway took a deep breath and went on, "Living conditions and level of technology should be similar to our own. Taxation might be high, but this would be negated by government controlled news channels. My guess is that this Empire has reached the unwieldy stage, say about forty to fifty inhabited systems . . ."

"Forty-three," said Williamson in a surprised voice.

". . . And I would guess that everyone in it knows about Etla and are sympathetic towards its plight. They would consider it a world under constant quarantine, but they do everything they can to help it . . ."

"They certainly do!" Williamson broke in. "Our man was on one of the outlying planets of the Empire for only two days before he was sent to the Central world for a audience with the Big Chief. But he had time to see what the people thought of Etla. There are pictures of the suffering Etlans practically everywhere he looked. In places they out-numbered commercial advertising, and it is a charity to which the

Imperial Government gives full support! These look like being very nice people, Doctor."

"I'm sure they are, Captain," Conway said savagely. "But don't you think it a trifle odd that the combined charity of forty-three inhabited systems can only run to sending one ship every ten years...?"

Williamson opened his mouth, closed it, and looked thoughtful. The whole room was silent except for the muted, incoming messages. Then suddenly, from behind Conway, Stillman swore and said thickly, "I see what he's getting at, sir. We've got to take off at once...!"

Williamson's eyes flicked from Conway to Stillman and back again. He murmured, "One could be temporary insanity, but two represents a trend..."

Three seconds later recall instructions were going out to all personnel, their urgency emphasised by the ear-splitting howl of the General Alarm siren. When every order which had been issued only minutes ago had been reversed, Williamson turned to Conway again.

"Go on, Doctor," he said grimly. "I think I'm beginning to see it, too."

Conway sighed thankfully and began to talk.

Etla had begun as a normal colony world, with a single spacefield to land the initial equipment and colonists, then towns had been set up convenient to natural resources and the planetary population had increased nicely. But then they must have been hit by a wave of disease, or a succession of diseases, which had threatened to wipe them out. Hearing of their plight the citizens of the Empire had rallied round, as people do when their friends are in trouble, and soon help began to arrive.

It must have started in a small way but built up quickly as news of the colony's distress got around. But so far as the Etlans were concerned the assistance stayed small.

The odd, un-missed pennies of a whole planetary population added up to a respectable amount, and when scores of worlds were contributing the amount was something which could not be ignored by the Imperial government, or by the Emperor himself. Because even in those days the Empire must have grown too big and the inevitable rot had set in at its core. More and more revenue was needed to maintain the Empire, and/or to maintain the Emperor and his court in the luxury to which they felt entitled. It was natural

70

to assume that they might tell themselves that charity began at home, and appropriate a large part of these funds for their own use. Then gradually, as the Etlan charity was publicised and encouraged, these funds became an essential part of the administration's income.

That was how it had begun.

Etla was placed in strict quarantine, even though nobody in their right mind would have wanted to go there anyway. But then a calamity threatened, the Etlans through their own unaided efforts must have begun to cure themselves. The lucrative source of revenue looked like drying up. Something had to be done, quickly.

From withholding the aid which would have cured them it was only a small matter ethically, the administration must have told itself, to keep the Etlans sick by introducing a few relatively harmless diseases from time to time. The diseases would have to be photogenic, of course, to have the maximum effect on the kind-hearted citizenry—disfiguring diseases, for the most part, or those which left the sufferer crippled or deformed. And steps had to be taken to ensure that the supply of suffering natives did not fall off, so that the techniques of gynaecology and child care on Etla were well advanced.

At a fairly early stage an Imperial Representative, psychologically tailored to fit his post, was installed to insure that the level of health on the planet was held at the desired point. Somehow the Etlans had ceased to be people and had become valuable sick animals, which was just how the Imperial Representative seemed to regard them.

Conway paused at that point. The Captain and Stillman were looking ill, he thought; which was exactly how he had felt since the destruction of Lonvellin's ship had caused all the pieces of the puzzle to fall into place.

He said, "A native force sufficient to drive off or destroy chance visitors is always at Teltrenn's disposal. Because of the quarantine all visitors are likely to be alien, and the natives have been taught to hate aliens regardless of shape, number or intentions . . ."

"But how could they be so . . . so cold-blooded?" Williamson said, aghast.

"It probably started as simple misappropriation of funds," Conway said tiredly, "then it gradually got out of hand. But now we, by our interference, have threatened to wreck a very

71

profitable Imperial racket. So now the Empire is trying to wreck us."

Before Williamson could reply the Chief Communications officer reported both helicopter crews back in the ship, also all personnel who had been within earshot of the siren, which meant everyone in town. The remainder could not make it back to *Vespasian* for several hours at least and had been ordered to go under cover until a scoutship sneaked in later to pick them up. Almost before the officer had finished speaking the Captain snapped "Lift ship" and Conway felt a moment's dizziness as the ship's anti-gravity grids compensated for full emergency thrust. *Vespasian* climbed frantically for space, with the courier vessel only ten seconds behind her.

"You must have thought me pretty stupid back there . . ." Williamson began, then was interrupted by reports from the returned crew-men. One of the helicopters had been fired on and the men from town had been ordered to stay there by the local police. These orders had come directly from the Imperial Representative, with instructions to kill anyone who tried to escape. But the local police and Corpsmen had come to know each other very well, and the Etlans had aimed well above their heads . . .

"This is getting dirtier by the minute," said Stillman suddenly. "You know, I think we are going to be blamed for what happened around Lonvellin's ship, for all the casualties in the area. Everything we have done here is going to be twisted so that *we* will be the villians. And I bet a lot of new diseases will be introduced immediately we leave, for which *we* will be blamed!"

Stillman swore, then went on, "You know how the people of the Empire think of this planet. Etla is their poor, weak, crippled sister, and we are going to be the dirty aliens who cold-bloodedly assaulted her . . ."

As the Major had been talking Conway had begun to sweat again. His deductions regarding the Empire's treatment of Etla had been from medical evidence, and it had been the medical aspect which had most concerned him, so that the larger implications of it all had not yet occurred to him. Suddenly he burst out, "But this could mean a *war!*"

"Yes indeed," said Stillman savagely, "and that is probably just what the Imperial government wants. It has grown too big and fat and rotten at the core, judging by what has been happening here. Within a few decades it would probably

72

fall apart of its own accord, and a good thing, too. But there is nothing like a good war, a Cause that everybody can feel strongly about, to pull a crumbling Empire together again. If they play it right *this* war could make it stand for another hundred years."

Conway shook his head numbly. "I should have seen what was happening sooner," he said. "If we'd had time to tell the Etlans the truth—"

"You saw it sooner than anyone else," the Captain broke in sharply, "and telling the natives would not have helped them or us if the ordinary people of the Empire could not have been told also. You have no reason to blame yourself for—"

"Ordnance Officer," said a voice from one of the twenty-odd speaker grills in the room. "We have a trace at Green Twelve Thirty-one which I'm putting on your repeater screen Five. Trace is putting out patterned interference against missile attack and considerable radar window, suggesting that it has a guilty conscience and is smaller than we are. Instructions, sir?"

Williamson glanced at the repeater screen. "Do nothing unless it does," he said, then turned to Stillman and Conway again. When he spoke it was with the calming, confidence-inspiring tone of the senior officer who bears, *and* accepts, full responsibility, a tone which insisted that they were not to worry because he was there to do it for them.

He said, "Don't look so distressed, gentlemen. This situation, this threat of interstellar war, was bound to come about sometime and plans have been devised for dealing with it. Luckily we have plenty of time to put these plans into effect.

"Spatially the Empire is a small, dense association of worlds," he went on reassuringly, "otherwise we could not have made contact with them so soon. The Federation, however, is spread thinly across half the Galaxy. We had a star cluster to search where one sun in five possessed an inhabited planet. Their problem is nowhere near as simple. If they were *very* lucky they might find us in three years, but my own estimate is that it would be nearer twenty. So you can see that we have plenty of time."

Conway did not feel reassured and he must have shown it, but the Captain was trying to meet his objections before he could make them.

"The agent who made the report may help them," Williamson went on quickly. "Willingly, because he doesn't know the truth about the Empire yet, he may give information regarding the Federation and the organisation and strength of its Monitor Corps. But because he is a doctor this information is unlikely to be either complete or accurate, and would be useless anyway unless the Empire knows where we are. They won't find that out unless they capture an astrogator or a ship with its charts intact, and that is a contingency which we will take very great precautions to guard against from this moment on.

"Agents are trained in linguistics, medicine or the social sciences," Williamson ended confidently. "Their knowledge of interstellar navigation is nil. The scoutship which lands them returns to base immediately, this being standard precautionary procedure in operations of this sort. So you can see that we have a serious problem but that it is not an immediate one."

"Isn't it?" said Conway.

He saw Williamson and Stillman looking at him—intently and cautiously as if he was some kind of bomb which, having exploded half an hour ago was about to do so again. In a way Conway was sorry that he had to explode on them again and make them share the fear and horrible, gnawing anxiety which up to now had been his alone. He wet his lips and tried to break it to them as gently as possible.

"Speaking personally," he said quietly, "I don't have the faintest idea of the coordinates of Traltha, or Illensa or Earth, or even the Earth-seeded planet where I was born. But there is one set of figures which I do know, and any other doctor on space service in this Sector is likely to know them also. They are the coordinates of Sector General.

"I don't think we have any time at all."

# Chapter Twelve

THE ONLY constructive thing which Conway did during the trip back to Sector General was to catch up on his sleep, but very often the sleep was made so hideous by nightmares of the coming war that it was more pleasant to stay awake, and his waking time he spent in discussions with Williamson, Stillman and the other senior officers on *Vespasian*. Since he had called the shots right during that last half hour on Etla Williamson seemed to value any ideas he might have, even though problems of espionage, logistics and fleet manoeuvres were hardly within the specialty of a Senior Physician.

The discussions were interesting, informative and, like his dreams, anything but pleasant.

According to Colonel Williamson an interstellar war of conquest was logistically impossible, but a simple war of extermination could be fought by anyone with sufficient force and stomachs strong enough to withstand the thought of slaughtering other intelligent beings by the planet-load. The Empire had more than enough force, and the strength of its collective stomach was dependent on factors over which the Monitor Corps had no control, *as yet*.

Given enough time agents of the Corps could have infiltrated the Empire. They already knew the position of one of its inhabited worlds and, because there was traffic between it and the other planets of the Empire, they would soon know the positions of others. The first step then would be to gather intelligence and eventually . . . Well, the Corps were no mean propagandists themselves and in a situation like this where the enemy was basing their campaign on a series of Big Lies, some method of striking at this weak spot could be devised. The Corps was primarily a police organisation, a force intended not so much to wage war as to maintain peace. And like any good police force its actions were constrained by the possible effects on innocent bystanders—in this case the citizens of the Empire as well as the people of the Federation.

That was why the plan for undermining the Empire would be set in motion, even though it could not possibly take effect before the first clash occurred. Williamson's fondest hope—or prayer might be a more accurate word—was that the Corpsman who was now in Empire hands would not know, and so would not be able to tell, the coordinates of Sector General. The Colonel was realist enough to know that if the agent knew anything the enemy would get it out of him one way or another. But failing this ideal solution the hospital would be defended in such a way that it would be the only Federation position that the enemy would know—unless they diverted a large proportion of their force to the time-wasting job of searching the main body of the Galaxy, which was just what the Corps wanted.

Conway tried not to think of what it would be like at Sector General when the entire mobile force of the Empire was concentrated there . . .

A few hours before emergence they received another report from the agent who was now on the Empire's Central World. The first one had taken nine days to reach Etla, the second was relayed with top priority coding in eighteen hours.

The report stated that the Central World did not seem to be as hostile towards extra-terrestrials as Etla and the other worlds of the Empire. The people there seemed much more cosmopolitan and occasionally e-ts could be seen in the streets. There were subtle indications, however, that beings had diplomatic status and were natives of worlds with which the Empire had made treaties with the purpose of holding them off as a group until such times as it could annex them individually. So far as the agent personally had been treated, things could not have been nicer, and in a few days time he was due for an audience with the Emperor himself. Nevertheless, he was beginning to feel uneasy.

It was nothing that he could put his finger on—he was a doctor who had been yanked off Survey and pre-Colonisation duty, he reminded them, and not one of the Cultural Contact hot-shots. He got the impression that on certain occasions and among certain people, all mention of the Federation's aims and constitution by himself was discouraged, while at other times, usually when there were only a few people present, they encouraged him to talk at great length. Another point which worried him was the fact that none of the newscasts he had seen made any mention of his arrival. Had the position been reversed and a citizen of the Empire made contact with the Federation, the event would have been top-line news for weeks.

He wondered sometimes if he was talking too much, and wished that a subspace receiver could be built as small as a sender so that he could ask for instructions . . .

That was the last they ever heard from that agent.

Conway's return to Sector General was not as pleasant as he had thought it would be a few weeks previously. Then he had expected to return as a near-heroic personage with the biggest assignment of his career successfully accomplished, the plaudits of his colleagues ringing in his ears and with Murchison waiting to receive him with open arms. The latter had been a very slim probability indeed, but Conway liked to dream sometimes. Instead he was returning from a job which had blown up most horribly in his face, hoping that his colleagues would not stop him to ask how or what he had been doing, and with Murchison standing inside the lock with a friendly smile on her face and both arms hanging correctly by her sides.

Meeting him after a long absence, Conway thought sourly, was the sort of thing one *friend* did for another—there could be nothing more to it than that. She said it was nice to see him back and he said it was nice to be back, and when she started to ask questions he said he had a lot of things to do now but would it be all right if he called her later, and he smiled as if calling her to arrange a date was the most important thing in his mind. But his smile had suffered through lack of use and she must have seen that there was something definitely insincere about it. She went all Doctor-and-Nurse on him, said that *of course* he had more important things to attend to, and left quickly.

Murchison had looked as beautiful and desirable as ever and he had undoubtedly hurt her feelings, but somehow none of these things mattered to Conway at the moment. His mind would not think of anything but his impending meeting with O'Mara. And when he presented himself in the office of the Chief Psychologist shortly afterwards it seemed that his worst forebodings were to be realised.

"Sit down, Doctor," O'Mara began. "So you finally succeeded in involving us in an interstellar war . . . ?"

"That isn't funny," said Conway.

O'Mara gave him a long, steady look. It was a look which not only noted the expression on Conway's face but such other factors as his posture in the chair and the position and movements of his hands. O'Mara did not set much store by correct modes of address, but the fact that Conway had omitted to say 'Sir' was also being noted as a contributory datum and given its proper place in his analysis of the situation. The process took perhaps two minutes and during that time the Chief Psychologist did not move an eyelid. O'Mara had no irritating mannerisms; his strong, blunt hands never twitched or fiddled with things, and when he desired it his features could be as expressive as a lump of rock.

On this occasion he let his face relax into an expression of almost benign disfavour, and finally he spoke.

"I agree," he said quietly, "it isn't a bit funny. But you know as well as I do that there is always the chance of some well-intentioned doctor in a place like this stirring up trouble on a large scale. We have often brought in some weird beastie of a hitherto unknown species who requires treatment urgently, and there is no time to search for its friends to discover if what we propose to do is the right procedure in the circumstances. A case in point was that Ian chrysalis you had a few months ago. That was before we made formal contact with the Ians, and if you hadn't correctly diagnosed the patient's condition as a growing chrysalis instead of a malignant growth requiring instant removal, a procedure which would have killed the patient, we would have been in serious trouble with the Ians."

"Yes, sir," said Conway.

O'Mara went on, "My remark was in the nature of a pleasantry, and had a certain aptness considering your recent experience with that Ian. Perhaps it was in questionable taste, but if you think I'm going to apologise then you obviously believe in miracles. Now tell me about Etla.

"And," he added quickly before Conway could speak, "my desk and wastebasket are full of reports detailing the implications and probable dire consequences of the Etla business. What I want to know is how you handled your assignment as originally given."

As briefly as possible Conway did as he was told. While he talked he felt himself begin to relax. He still had a confused and very frightening picture in the back of his mind of what the war would mean to countless millions of beings, to the hospital and to himself, but he no longer felt that he was partly responsible for bringing it about. O'Mara had begun the interview by accusing him of the very thing he had felt guilty of, then without saying so in so many words had made him see how ridiculous it had been to feel guilty. But as he neared the point where Lonvellin's ship had been destroyed, the feeling returned full strength. If he had put the pieces together sooner, Lonvellin would not have died . . .

O'Mara must have detected the change of feeling, but allowed him to finish before he said, "It surprises me that

Lonvellin didn't see it before you did, it being the brain behind the operation. And while we're on the subject of brains, yours does not seem to be thrown into complete disorder by problems involving large numbers of people requiring differing forms of treatment. So I have another job for you. It is smaller than the Etla assignment, you won't have to leave the hospital, and with any luck it won't blow up in your face."

"I want you to organise the evacuation of Sector General."

Conway swallowed, then swallowed again.

"Stop looking as though you'd been sandbagged!" O'Mara said testily, "or I *will* hit you with something! You must have thought this thing through far enough to see that we can't have patients here when the Empire force arrives. Or any non-military staff who have not volunteered to stay. Or *any* person, regardless of position or rank, who has in his mind detailed information regarding the whereabouts of any Federation planets. And surely the idea of telling people nominally your superiors what to do doesn't frighten you, not after ordering a Corps Colonel around . . ."

Conway felt his neck getting warm. He let the dig about Williamson pass and said, "I thought we might leave the place empty for them."

"No," said O'Mara drily. "It has too much sentimental, monetary and strategic value. We hope to keep a few levels operating for the treatment of casualties sustained by the defending force. Colonel Skempton is already at work on the evacuation problem and will help you all he can. What time is it by you, Doctor?"

Conway told him that when he had left *Vespasian* it had been two hours after breakfast.

"Good," said O'Mara. "You can contact Skempton and go to work at once. With me it is long past bedtime, but I'll sleep here in case you or the Colonel want something. Goodnight, Doctor."

So saying he took off and folded his tunic, stepped out of his shoes and lay down. Within seconds his breathing became deep and regular. Suddenly Conway laughed.

"Seeing the Chief Psychologist lying on his own couch," Conway said through his laughter, "is something of a traumatic experience. I very much doubt, sir, if our relationship will ever be quite the same . . ."

As he was leaving O'Mara murmured sleepily, "I'm glad. For a while there I thought you were going all melancholy on me..."

## Chapter Thirteen

SEVEN HOURS later Conway surveyed his littered desk wearily but with a measure of triumph, rubbed his eyes and looked across at the desk facing his. For a moment he felt that he was back on Etla and that a red-eyed Major Stillman would look up and ask what he wanted. But it was a red-eyed Colonel Skempton who looked up when he spoke.

"The breakdown of patients to be evacuated is complete," Conway said tiredly. "There are divided first into species, which will indicate the number of ships required to move them and the living conditions which must be reproduced in each ship. With some of the weirder types this will necessitate structural alterations to the vessels, which will take time. Then each species is sub-divided into degrees of seriousness of the patient's condition, which will determine the order of their going..."

Except, thought Conway sourly, when a patient's condition was such that to move it would endanger its life. In which case it would have to be evacuated last instead of first so that treatment could be prolonged as much as possible, which meant that specialised medical staff who themselves should have been evacuated by that time would be held back to treat it, and by that time its life might be endangered by missiles from an Empire warship anyway. *Nothing* seemed to happen in a tidy, consecutive fashion anymore.

"...Then it will take a few days for Major O'Mara's department to process the medical and maintenance staff," Conway went on, "even though he just has to ask them a few questions under scop. When I arrived I expected the hospital to be under attack already. At the moment I don't know whether to plan for a panic evacuation within forty-eight hours, which is the absolute minimum time for it and which would probably kill more patients than it would save, or take my time and plan for a merely hurried evacuation."

"I couldn't assemble the transport in forty-eight hours," said Skemptom shortly, and lowered his head again. As Chief of Maintenance and the Hospital's ranking Monitor officer the job of assembling, modifying and routing the transports devolved on him, and he had an awful lot of work to do.

"What I'm trying to say," Conway said insistently, "is how much time do you think we've got?"

The Colonel looked up again. "Sorry, Doctor," he said. "I have an estimate which came in a few hours ago..." He lifted one of the top layer of papers on his desk and began to read.

Subjecting all the known factors to a rigid analysis, the report stated, it appeared likely that a short time-lag would occur between the point at which the Empire discovered the exact position of Sector General and the time when they acted on this information. The initial action was likely to be an investigation by a scoutship or a small scouting force. Monitor units at present stationed around Sector General would attempt to destroy this force. Whether they were successful or not the Empire's next move would be more decisive, probably a full-scale offensive which would require many days to mount. By that time additional units of the Monitor Corps would have reached the area...

"... Say eight days," Skempton concluded, "or three weeks if we're lucky. But I don't think we'll be lucky."

"Thank you," said Conway, and returned to work.

First he prepared an outline of the situation for distribution to the medical staff within the next six hours. In it he laid as much stress as possible on the necessity for a quick, orderly evacuation without overdoing it to the extent of causing a panic, and recommended that patients be informed via their physicians so as to cause the minimum distress. In the case of seriously ill patients the doctors in charge should use their discretion whether the patient should be told or evacuated under sedation. He added that an at present unspecified number of medical staff would be evacuated with the patients and that everyone should be prepared to leave the hospital at a few hours notice. This document he sent to Publications for copying in print and tape so that everyone would be in possession of the information at roughly the same time.

At least that was the theory, Conway thought drily. But

if he knew his hospital grape-vine the essential data would be circulating ten minutes after it left his desk.

Next he prepared more detailed instructions regarding the patients. The warm-blooded oxygen-breathing life-forms could leave by any of several levels, but the heavy-G, high-pressure species would pose special problems, not to mention the light-gravity MSVKs and LSVOs, the giant, water-breathing AUGLs, the ultra-frigid types and the dozen or so beings on Level Thirty-eight who breathed superheated steam. Conway was planning on the operation taking five days for the patients and an additional two for the staff, and for this rapid clearing of the wards he would have to send people through levels foreign to them to reach their embarkation points. There would be possible oxygen contamination of chlorine environments, danger of chlorine leaking into the AUGL wards, or of water flooding all over the place. Precautions would have to be taken against failure of the methane life-forms' refrigerators, breakdown of the anti-gravity equipment of the fragile, bird-like LSVOs and rupture of Illensan pressure envelopes.

Contamination was the greatest danger in a multi-environment hospital—contamination by oxygen, chlorine, methane, water, cold, heat or radiation. During the evacuation the safety devices usually in operation—airtight doors, double, inter-level locks, the various detection and alarm systems—would have to be overridden in the interests of a quick get-away.

Then staff would have to be detailed to inspect the transport units to ensure that their passenger space accurately reproduced the environment of the patients they were to carry . . .

All at once Conway's mind refused to take any more of it. He closed his eyes, sank his head into the palms of his hands and watched the after-image of his desk-top fade slowly into redness. He was sick of paperwork. Since being given the Etla job his whole life had been paperwork; reports, summaries, charts, instructions. He was a doctor currently planning a complicated operation, but it was the sort of operation performed by a high-level clerk rather than a surgeon. Conway had not studied and trained for the greater part of his life to be a clerk.

He stood up, excused himself hoarsely to the Colonel and

left the office. Without really thinking about it he was moving in the direction of his wards.

A new shift was just coming on duty and to the patients it was half an hour before the first meal of the day, which made it a very unusual time for a Senior Physician to do his rounds. The mild panic he caused would, in other circumstances, have been funny. Conway greeted the intern on duty politely, felt mildly surprised to find that it was the Creppelian octopoid he had met as a trainee two months previously, then felt annoyed when the AMSL insisted on following him around at a respectful distance. This was the proper procedure for a junior intern, but at that moment Conway wanted to be alone with his patients and his thoughts.

Most strongly of all he felt the need to see and speak to the sometimes weird and always wonderful extra-terrestrial patients who were technically under his care—all the beings he had come to know before leaving for Etla having been long since discharged. He did *not* look at their charts, however, because he had an allergy towards the abstraction of information via the printed word at the moment. Instead he questioned them closely, almost hungrily, regarding their symptoms and condition and background. He left some of the minor cases pleased and flabberghasted by such attention from a Senior Physician, and some might have been annoyed by his prying. But Conway had to do it. While he still had patients left he wanted to be a doctor.

An *e-t* doctor . . .

Sector General was breaking up. The vast, complex structure dedicated to the relief of suffering and the advance of xenological medicine was dying, succumbing like any terminal patient to a disease too powerful for it to resist. Tomorrow or the next day these wards would begin to empty. The patients with their exotic variations of physiology, metabolism and complaints would drain away. In darkened wards the weird and wonderful fabrications which constituted the alien idea of a comfortable bed would crouch like surrealistic ghosts along the walls. And with the departure of the e-t patients and staff would go the necessity for maintaining the environments which housed them, the Translators which allowed them to communicate, the physiology tapes which made it possible for one species to treat another . . .

But the Galaxy's greatest e-t hospital would not die completely, not for another few days or weeks. The Monitor Corps had no experience of interstellar wars, this being their first, but they thought they knew what to expect. Casualties among the ship's crews would be heavy and with a very high proportion of them fatal. The still-living casualties brought in would be of three types; decompression, bone-fractures and radiation poisoning. It was expected that two or three levels would be enough to take care of them, because if the engagement was fought with nuclear weapons, and there was no reason to suppose otherwise, most of the decompression and fracture cases would be radiation-terminal also—there would be no danger of overcrowding.

Then the internal break-up began with the evacuation would continue on the structural level as the Empire forces attacked. Conway was no military tactician, but he could not see how the vast, nearly-empty hospital could be protected. It was a sitting duck, soon to be a dead one. A great, fused and battered metal graveyard . . .

All at once a tremendous wave of feeling washed through Conway's mind—bitterness, sadness and a surge of sheer anger which left him shaking. As he stumbled out of the ward he didn't know whether he wanted to cry or curse or knock somebody down. But the decision was taken away from him when he turned the corner leading to the PVSJ section and collided solidly with Murchison.

The impact was not painful, one of the colliding bodies being well endowed with shock-absorbing equipment, but it was sharp enough to jolt his mind of a very sombre train of thought onto one infinitely more pleasant. Suddenly he wanted to watch and talk to Murchison as badly as he had wanted to visit his patients, and for the same reason. This might be the last time he would see her.

"I—I'm sorry," he stammered, backing off. Then remembering their last meeting, he said, "I was a bit rushed at the lock this morning, couldn't say much. Are you on duty?"

"Just coming off," said Murchison in a neutral voice.

"Oh," said Conway, then; "I wondered if . . . that is, would you mind . . ."

"I wouldn't mind going for a swim," she said.

"Fine," said Conway.

They went up to the recreation level, changed and met inside on the simulated beach. While they were walking towards the water she said suddenly, "Oh, Doctor. When you were sending me those letters, did you ever think of putting them in envelopes with my name and room number on them?"

"And let everybody know I was writing to you?" Conway said. "I didn't think you wanted that."

Murchison gave a lady-like snort. "The system you devised was not exactly secret," she said with a hint of anger in her tone. "Thornnastor in Pathology has three mouths and it can't keep any of them shut. They were nice letters, but I don't think it was fitting for you to write them on the back of sputum test reports . . . !"

"I'm sorry," said Conway. "It won't happen again."

With the words the dark mood which the sight of Murchison had pushed from his mind came rushing back. It certainly wouldn't happen again, he thought bleakly, not ever. And the hot, artificial sun did not seem to be warming his skin as he remembered it and the water was not so stingingly cold. Even in the half-G conditions the swim was wearying rather than exhilarating. It was as if some deep layer of tiredness swathed his body, dulling all sensation. After only a few minutes he returned to the shallows and waded onto the beach. Murchison followed him, looking concerned.

"You've got thinner," she said when she had caught up with him.

Conway's first impulse was to say "You haven't," but the intended compliment could have been taken another way, and he was lousy enough company already without running the risk of insulting her. Then he had an idea and said quickly, "I forgot that you're just off duty and haven't eaten yet. Will we go to the restaurant?"

"Yes, *please*," said Murchison.

The restaurant was perched high on the cliff facing the diving ledges and boasted a continuous transparent wall which allowed a full view of the beach while keeping out the noise. It was the only place in the recreation level where quiet conversation was possible. But the quietness was wasted on them because they hardly spoke at all.

Until half way through the meal when Murchison said, "You aren't eating as much, either."

Conway said, "Have you ever owned, or navigated, a space vessel?"

"*Me?* Of course not!"

"Or if you were wrecked in a ship whose astrogator

was injured and unconscious," he persisted, "and the ship's drive had been repaired, could you give the coordinates for reaching some planet within the Federation?"

"No," said Murchison impatiently. "I'd have to stay there until the astrogator woke up. What sort of questions are these?"

"The sort I'll be asking all my friends," Conway replied grimly. "If you had answered 'Yes' to one of them it would have taken a load off my mind."

Murchison put down her knife and fork, frowning slightly. Conway thought that she looked lovely when she frowned, or laughed, or did anything. Especially when she was wearing a swimsuit. That was one thing he liked about this place, they allowed you to dine in swimsuits. And he wished that he could pull himself out of his dismal mood and be sparkling company for a couple of hours. On his present showing he doubted if Murchison would let him take her home, much less co-operate in the clinch for the two minutes, forty-eight seconds it took for the robot to arrive...

"Something is bothering you," Murchison said. She hesitated, then went on, "If you need a soft shoulder, be my guest. But remember it is only for crying on, nothing else."

"What else could I use it for?" said Conway.

"I don't know," she said, smiling, "but I'd probably find out."

Conway did not smile in return. Instead he began to talk about the things that were worrying him—and the people, including her. When he had finished she was quiet for a long time. Sadly Conway watched the faintly ridiculous picture of a young, dedicated, very beautiful girl in a white swimsuit coming to a decision which would almost certainly cost her her life.

"I think I'll stay behind," she said finally, as Conway knew she would. "You're staying too, of course?"

"I haven't decided yet," Conway said carefully. "I can't leave until after the evacuation anyway. And there may be nothing to stay for..." He made a last try to make her change her mind. "...and all your e-t training would be wasted. There are lots of other hospitals that would be glad to have you..."

Murchison sat up straight in her seat. When she spoke it was in the brisk, competent, no-nonsense tone of a nurse prescribing treatment to a possibly recalcitrant patient. She said, "From what you tell me you're going to have a busy day tomorrow. You should get all the sleep you can. In fact, I think you should go to your room right away."

Then in a completely different tone she added, "But if you'd like to take me home first..."

# Chapter Fourteen

ON THE day after instructions to evacuate the hospital had been issued, everything went smoothly. The patients gave no trouble at all, the natural order of things being for patients to leave hospital and in this instance their discharge was just a little bit more dramatic than usual. Discharging the medical staff, however, was a most unnatural thing. To a patient Hospital was merely a painful, or at least not very pleasant, episode in his life. To the staff of Sector General the hospital *was* their life.

Everything went smoothly with the staff on the first day also. Everyone did as they were told, probably because habit and their state of shock made that the easiest thing to do. But by the second day the shock had worn off and they began to produce arguments, and the person they most wanted to argue with was Dr. Conway.

On the third day Conway had to call O'Mara.

"What's the trouble!" Conway burst out when O'Mara replied. "The trouble is making this ... this gaggle of geniuses see things sensibly! And the brighter a being is the more stupid it insists on acting. Take Prilicla, a beastie who is so much egg-shell and match-sticks that it would blow away in a strong draught, *it* wants to stay. And Doctor Mannen, who is as near being a Diagnostician as makes no difference. Mannen says treating exclusively human casualties would be something of a holiday. And the reasons some of the others have thought up are fantastic."

"You've got to make them see sense, sir. You're the Chief Psychologist..."

"Three quarters of the medical and maintenance staff," O'Mara said sharply, "are in possession of information likely to help the enemy in the event of their capture. They will be leaving, regardless of whether they are Diagnosticians, computermen or junior ward orderlies, for reasons of security. They will have no choice in the matter. In addition to these there will be a number of specialist medical staff who will feel obliged, because of their patient's condition, to travel with their charges. So far as the remainder are concerned there is very little I can do, they are sane, intelligent, mature beings capable of making up their own minds."

Conway said, "Hah."

"Before you impugn other people's sanity," O'Mara said drily, "answer me one question. Are *you* going to stay?"

"Well . . ." began Conway.

O'Mara broke the connection.

Conway stared at the handset a long time without reclipping it. He still had not made up his mind if he was going to stay or not. He knew that he wasn't the heroic type, and he badly wanted to leave. But he didn't want to leave without his friends, because if Murchison and Prilicla and the others stayed behind, he couldn't have borne the things they would think about him if he was to run away.

Probably they all thought that he meant to stay but was being coy about it, while the truth was that he was too cowardly and at the same time too much of a hypocrite to admit to them that he was afraid . . .

The sharp voice of Colonel Skemptom broke into his mood of self-loathing, dispelling it for the moment.

"Doctor, the Kelgian hospital ship is here. And an Illensan freighter. Locks Five and Seventeen in ten minutes."

"Right," said Conway. He left the office at a near run, heading for Reception.

All three control desks were occupied when he arrived, two by Nidians and the other by a Corps Lieutenant on stand-by. Conway positioned himself between and behind the Nidians where he could study both sets of repeater screens and began hoping very hard that he could deal with the things which would inevitably go wrong.

The Kelgian vessel already locked on at Five was a brute, one of the latest interstellar liners which had been partially converted into a hospital ship on the way out. The alterations were not quite complete, but a team of maintenance staff and robots were already boarding it together with senior ward staff who would arrange for the disposition of their patients. At the same time the occupants of the wards were being readied for the transfer and the equipment necessary for treating them was being dismantled, rapidly and with little regard for the subsequent condition of the ward walls. Some of the smaller equipment, heaped onto powered stretcher-carriers, was already on the way to the ship.

Altogether it looked like being a fairly simple operation. The atmosphere, pressure and gravity requirement of the patients were exactly those of the ship, so that no complicated protective arrangements were necessary, and the vessel was big enough to take all of the Kelgian patients with room to spare. He would be able to clear the DBLF levels completely *and* get rid of a few Tralthan FGLIs as well. But even though the first job was relatively uncomplicated, Conway estimated that it would take at least six hours for the ship to be loaded and away. He turned to the other control desk.

Here the picture was in many respects similar. The environment of the Illensan freighter matched perfectly that of the PVSJ wards, but the ship was smaller and, considering its purpose, did not have a large crew. The preparations for receiving patients aboard were, for this reason, not well advanced. Conway directed extra maintenance staff to the Illensan freighter, thinking that they would be lucky to get away with sixty PVSJs in the same time as it took the other ship to clear three whole levels.

He was still trying to find short-cuts in the problem when the Lieutenant's screen lit up.

"A Tralthan ambulance ship, Doctor," he reported. "Fully staffed and with provision for six FROBs and a Chalder as well as twenty of their own species. No preparation needed at their end, they say just load 'em up."

The AUGL denizens of Chalderescol, a forty-foot long, armoured fish-like species were water-breathers who could not live in any other medium for more than a few seconds and live. On the other hand the FROBs were squat, immensely massive and thick-skinned beings accustomed to the crushing gravity and pressure of Hudlar. Properly speaking Hudlarians did not breathe at all, and their incredibly strong tegument allowed them to exist for long periods in conditions of zero gravity and pressure, so that the water in the AUGL section would not bother them ...

Conway said quickly, "Lock Twenty-eight for the Chalder. While they're loading it send the FROBs through the ELNT section into the main AUGL tank and out by the same Lock. Then tell them to move to Lock Five and we'll have their other patients waiting . . ."

Gradually the evacuation got under way. Accommodations was prepared for the first convalescent PVSJs aboard the Illensan freighter and the slow trek of patients and staff through the noisome yellow fog of the chlorine section commenced. Simultaneously the other screen was showing a long, undulating file of Kelgians moving towards their ship, with medical and engineering staff carrying equipment charging up and down the line.

To some it might have seemed callous to evacuate the convalescent patients first, but there were very good reasons for doing so. With these walking wounded out of the way the wards and approaches to the locks would be less congested, which would allow the complicated frames and harnesses containing the more seriously ill patients to be moved more easily, as well as giving them a little more time in the optimum conditions of the wards.

"Two more Illensan ships, Doctor," the lieutenant said suddenly. "Small jobs, capacity about twenty patients each."

"Lock Seventeen is still tied up," said Conway. "Tell them to orbit."

The next arrival was a small passenger ship from the Earth-human world of Gregory, and with it came the lunch trays. There were only a few Earth-human patients at Sector General, but at a pinch the Gregorian ship could take any warm-blooded oxygen-breather below the mass of a Tralthan. Conway dealt with both arrivals at the same time, not caring if he *did* have to speak or even shout, with his mouth full . . .

Then suddenly the sweating, harassed face of Colonel Skempton flicked onto the internal screen. He said sharply, "Doctor, there are two Illensan ships hanging about in orbit. Don't you have work for them?"

"Yes!" said Conway, irritated by the other's tone. "But there is a ship already loading chlorine-breathers at Seventeen, and there is no other lock suitable on that level. They'll have to wait their turn . . ."

"That won't do," Skempton cut in harshly. "While they're hanging about out there they are in danger should the enemy attack suddenly. Ether you start loading them at once or we send them away to come back later. Probably much later. Sorry."

Conway opened his mouth and then shut it with a click over what he had been about to say. Hanging grimly onto his temper he tried to think.

He knew that the build-up of the defence fleet had been going on for days and that the astrogation officers responsible for bringing those units in would leave again as soon as possible—either on their own scoutships or with the patients leaving Sector General. The plan devised by the Monitor Corps called for no information regarding the whereabouts of the Federation being available in the minds of the defending forces or the non-combatants who remained in the hospital. The defence fleet was deployed to protect the hospital and the ships locked on to it, and the thought of two other ships swinging around loose, ships which contained fully qualified astrogators aboard, must have made the Monitor fleet commander start biting his nails.

"Very well, Colonel," Conway said. "We'll take the ships at Fifteen and Twenty-one. This will mean chlorine-breathers travelling through the DBLF maternity ward and a part of the AUGL section. Despite these complications we should have the patients aboard in three hours . . ."

*Complications was right . . !* Conway thought grimly as he gave the necessary orders. Luckily both the DBLF ward and that section of the AUGL level would be vacant by the time the chlorine-breathing Illensans in their pressure tents came through. But the ship from Gregory was at an adjoining lock taking on ELNTs who were being shepherded through the area by DBLF nurses in protective suits. Also there were some of the low-G, bird-like MSVKs being brought to the same vessel through the chlorine ward which he was hoping to clear . . .

There weren't enough screens in Reception to keep properly in touch with what was going on down there, Conway decided suddenly. He had the horrible feeling that a most awful snarl-up would occur if he wasn't careful. But he couldn't be careful if he didn't know what was going on. The only course was for him to go there and direct the traffic himself.

He called O'Mara, explained the situation quickly and asked for a relief.

# *Chapter Fifteen*

DR. MANNEN arrived, groaned piteously at the battery of screens and flashing lights, then smoothly took over the job of directing the evacuation. As a replacement Conway could not have hoped for anyone better. He was turning to go when Mannen pushed his face within three inches of one of the screens and said "Harrumph."

Conway stopped. "What's wrong?"

"Nothing, nothing," said Mannen, without turning round. "It's just that I'm beginning to understand why you want to go down there."

"But I told you why!" said Conway impatiently. He stamped out, telling himself angrily that Mannen was indulging in senseless conversation at a time when unnecessary talk of any kind was criminal. Then he wondered if the ageing Dr. Mannen was tired, or had a particularly confusing tape riding him, and felt suddenly ashamed. Snapping at Skempton or the receptionists hadn't worried him unduly, but he did not want to begin biting the heads off his friends—even if he was harassed and tired and the whole place was rapidly going to Hell on horseback. Then very soon he was being kept too busy to feel ashamed.

Three hours later the state of confusion around him seemed to have doubled, although in actual fact it was simply that twice as much was being accomplished twice as fast. From his position at one of the high-level entrances to the main AUGL ward Conway could look down on a line of ELNTs—six-legged, crab-like entities from Melf IV—scuttling or being towed across the floor of the great tank. Unlike their amphibious patients, the thickly-furred, air breathing Kelgians attending them had to wear protective envelopes which were sweltering hot inside. The scraps of Translated conversation which drifted up to him, although necessarily emotionless, verged on the incandescent. But the work was being done, and much faster than Conway had ever hoped for.

In the corridor behind him a slow procession of Illensans, some in protective suits and the more seriously ill in pressure tents which enclosed their beds, moved past. They were being attended by Earth-human and Kelgian nurses. The transfer was going smoothly now, but there had been a time only half an hour back when Conway had wondered if it would go at all...

When the large pressure tents came through into the water-filled AUGL section they had risen like giant chlorine bubbles and stuck fast against the ceiling. Towing them along the corridor ceiling had been impossible because outgrowths of plumbing might have ruptured the thin envelopes, and getting five or six nurses to weigh them down was impractical. And when he brought in powered stretcher carriers from the level above—vehicles not designed for but theoretically capable of operating under water—with the idea of both holding his super-buoyant patients down and moving them quickly, a battery casing had split and the carrier became the centre of a mass of hissing, bubbling water which had rapidly turned black.

Conway would not be surprised to hear that the patient on that particular carrier had a relapse.

He had solved the problem finally with a magnificent flash of inspiration which, he told himself disgustedly, should have come two seconds after he had seen the problem. He had quickly switched the artificial gravity grids in the corridor to zero attraction and in the weightless condition the pressure tents had lost their buoyancy. It meant that the nurses had to swim instead of walk with their patients, but that was a small thing.

It was during the transfer of these PVSJs that Conway learned the reason for Mannen's 'Harrumph' up in Reception—Murchison was one of the nurses on that duty. She hadn't recognised him, of course, but he knew there was only one person who could fill a nurse's lightweight suit the way she did. He didn't speak to her, however—it didn't seem to be the proper time or place.

Time passed rapidly without another major crisis developing. At Lock Five the Kelgian hospital ship was ready to go, waiting only for some of the hospital's senior staff to go aboard and for a Monitor ship to escort them out to a safe jump distance. Remembering some of the beings who were scheduled to leave on that ship, many of them friends of long standing, Conway decided the chance offered by the quiet spell to say a quick good-bye to some of them. He called Mannen to tell him where he was going, then headed for Five.

But by the time he arrived the Kelgian ship had gone. In one of the big direction vision panels he could see it drawing away with a Monitor cruiser in close attendance; and beyond them, hanging like newly-formed constellations in the blackness, lay the Monitor defence fleet. The buildup of units around the hospital was proceeding as planned and had increased visibly since Conway had looked at it yesterday. Reassured, and not a little awed by the sight, he hurried back to the AUGL section.

And arrived to find the corridor almost plugged by an expanding sphere of ice.

The ship from Gregory contained a specially refrigerated compartment for beings of the SNLU classification. These were fragile, crystalline, methane-based life-forms who would be instantly cremated if the temperature rose above minus one-twenty. Sector General was currently treating seven of these ultra-frigid creatures, and all of them had been packed into a ten-foot refrigerated sphere for the transfer. Because of the difficulties expected in handling them they were the last patients for the Gregorian ship.

If there had been a direct opening to space from the cold section they would have been moved to the ship along the outer hull, but as this was not possible they had to be brought through fourteen levels from the methane ward to their loading point at Lock Sixteen. In all the other levels the corridors had been spacious and filled with air or chlorine, so that all that the protective sphere had done was to collect a coating of frost and chill the surrounding atmosphere. But in the AUGL section it was growing ice. Fast.

Conway had known this would happen but had not considered it important because the sphere should not have been in the water-filled corridor long enough to cause a problem. But one of the towing lines had snapped and pulled it against some projecting conduit and within seconds they were welded together with ice. Now the sphere was encased in an icy shell four feet thick and there was barely room to pass above or below it.

"Get cutting torches down here," Conway bawled up to Mannen, "quick!"

Three Corpsmen arrived just before the corridor was completely blocked. With the cutting flames of their torches set to maximum dispersal they attacked the icy mass, melting it free of the projection and trying to reduce it to a more managable size. In the confined space of the corridor the heat being applied to the ice-ball sent the water temperature soaring up, and none of their suits had cooling units. Conway began to feel a distinct empathy towards boiled lobsters. And the great, awkward mass of ice was a danger to life and limb—danger from being crushed between it and the corridor wall, and the scalding, nearly opaque water which made it so easy to put an arm or leg between the ice and a cutting flame.

But finally the job was done. The container with its SNLU occupants was manoevured through the inter-level lock into another air-filled section. Conway rubbed a hand across the outside of his helmet in an unconscious attempt to wipe the sweat from his forehead and wondered what else would go wrong.

The answer, according to Dr. Mannen up in Reception, was not a thing.

All three levels of DBLF patients had left with the Kelgian ship, Mannen told him enthusiastically, the only caterpillars remaining in the hospital being a few of the nursing staff. Between them the three Illensan freighters had cleared the PVSJ wards of their chlorine-breathers, except for a few stragglers who would be aboard within a few minutes. Among the water-breathing types the AUGLs and ELNTs were clear, and the SNLUs in their baby ice-berg were just going aboard. In all fourteen levels had been cleared and that was not a bad day's work. Dr. Mannen suggested that Dr. Conway might take this opportunity of applying a pillow to his head and going into a state of voluntary unconsciousness in preparation for an equally busy day tomorrow.

Conway was swimming tiredly towards the inter-level lock, his mind revolving around the infinitely alluring concepts of a large steak and a long sleep, when it happened.

Something which he did not see struck him a savage, disabling blow. It hit simultaneously in the abdomen, chest and legs—the places where his suit was tightest. Agony burst inside him like a red explosion that was just barely contained by his tortured body. He doubled up and began to black out, he wanted to die and he desperately wanted to be sick. But

95

some tiny portion of his brain unaffected by the pain and nausea insisted that he did not allow himself to be sick, that being sick inside his helmet was a very *nasty* way to die . . .

Gradually the pain receded and became bearable. Conway still felt as if a Tralthan had kicked him in the groin with all six feet, but other things were beginning to register. Loud, insistent, gurgling noises and the extremely odd sight of a Kelgian drifting in the water without its protective suit. A second look told him that it was wearing a suit, but that it was ruptured and full of water.

Further down in the AUGL tank two more Kelgians floated, their long, soft, furry bodies burst open from head to tail, the ghastly details mercifully obscured by an expanding red fog. And against the opposite wall of the tank there was an area of turbulence around a dark, irregular hole through which the water seemed to be leaving.

Conway swore. He thought he knew what had happened. Whatever had made that ragged-edged hole had, because of the non-compressibility of water, also expended its force on the unfortunate occupants of the AUGL tank. But because the other Kelgian and himself had been up here in the corridor they had escaped the worst effects of it.

Or maybe only one of them had escaped . . .

It took three minutes for him to drag the Kelgian nurse into the lock ten yards along the corridor. Once inside he set the pumps going to clear the chamber of water, simultaneously cracking an air valve. While the last of the water was draining away he struggled to lay the sodden, inert body on its side against one wall. The being's silvery pelt was a mass of dirty grey spikes, and he could detect no pulse or respiration. Conway quickly lay down on his side on the floor, moved the third and fourth set of legs apart so that he could put his shoulder into the space between them, then with his own feet braced firmly against the opposite wall he began to push rhythmically. Sitting on top of it and pressing down with the palms was not, Conway knew, an effective method of applying artificial respiration to one of the massive DBLFs. After a few seconds water began trickling out of its mouth.

He broke off suddenly as he heard somebody trying to open the lock from the AUGL corridor side. Conway tried his radio, but one or the other of their sets was not working. Taking off his helmet quickly he put his mouth up against the seal, cupped his hands around it and yelled, "I've an air-breather in here without its suit, don't open the seal or you'll drown us! Come in from the other side ... !"

A few minutes later the seal on the air-filled side opened and Murchison was looking down at him. She said, "D-Doctor Conway ..." in a peculiar voice.

Conway straightened his legs sharply, ramming his shoulder into the area of the Kelgian's underbelly nearest its lungs and said, "What?"

"I ... You ... the explosion ..." she began. Then after the brief false start her tone became firm and purposeful as she went on, "There's been an explosion, Doctor. One of the DBLF nurses is injured, severe lacerated wounds caused by a piece of floor plating spinning against it. We coagulated at once but I don't think its holding. And the corridor where its lying is being flooded, the explosion must have opened a way into the AUGL section. The air-pressure is dropping slightly so we must be open to space somewhere, too, and there is a distinct smell of chlorine ..."

Conway groaned and ceased his efforts with the Kelgian, but before he could speak Murchison went on quickly, "All the Kelgian doctors have been evacuated and the only DBLFs left are this one and a couple who should be around here somewhere, but they're just nursing staff ..."

Here was a proper mess, Conway thought as he scrambled to his feet; contamination *and* threatening decompression. The injured being would have to be moved quickly, because if the pressure dropped too much the airtight doors would drop and if the patient was on the wrong side of them when they did it would be just too bad. And the absence of a qualified DBLF meant that he would have to take a Kelgian physiology tape and do the job himself, which meant a quick trip to O'Mara's office. But first he would have to look at the patient.

"Take over this one, please Nurse," he said, indicating the sodden mass on the floor, "I think it's beginning to breath for itself, but will you give it another ten minutes ..." He watched while Murchison lay down on her side, knees bent and with both feet planted against the opposite wall. This was definitely neither the time nor the place, but the sight of her lying there in that demoralisingly tight suit made the urgency of patients, evacuations and physiology tapes diminish for just an instant. Then the tight, moisture beaded suit made him remember that Murchison had been in the AUGL tank, too, just a few minutes before the explosion, and he had an awful vision of her lovely body burst open like those of the two hapless DBLFs ...

"Between the third and fourth pair of legs, not the fifth and sixth!" Conway said harshly as he turned to go.

Which wasn't what he had meant to say at all.

## Chapter Sixteen

FOR SOME reason Conway's mind had been considering the effects of the explosion rather than its cause. Or perhaps he had been deliberately trying not to think along that line, trying to fool himself that there had been some sort of accident rather than that the hospital was under attack. But the yammering PA reminded him of the truth at every intersection and on the way to O'Mara's office everyone was moving twice as fast as usual and, as usual, all in a direction opposite to Conway's. He wondered if they all felt as he did, scared, unprotected, momentarily expecting a second explosion to rip the floor apart under their hurrying feet. Yet it was stupid of him to hurry because he might be rushing towards the spot where the next explosion would occur ...

He had to force himself to walk slowly into the Chief Psychologist's office, detail his requirements and ask O'Mara quietly what had happened.

"Seven ships," O'Mara replied, motioning Conway onto the couch as he lowered the Educator helmet into position. "They seem to have been small jobs, with no evidence of unusual armament or defences. There was quite a scrap. Three got away and one of the four which didn't launched a missile at us before it was clobbered. A small missile with a chemical warhead.

"Which is very odd," O'Mara went on thoughtfully, "because if it had been a nuclear warhead there would be no hospital here now. We weren't expecting them just as soon as this and were taken by surprise a little. Do you have to take this patient?"

"Eh? Oh, yes," said Conway. "You know DBLF. Any incised wound is an emergency with them. By the time another doctor had a look at the patient and came up here for a tape it might be too late."

OMara grunted. His hard, square, oddly gentle hands checked the fitting of the helmet, then pressed Conway down onto the couch. He went on, "They tried to press that attack home, it was really vicious. A clear indication, I would say, of their feelings toward us. Yet they used a chemical head when they could have destroyed us completely. Peculiar. One thing, though, it has made the ditherers make up their minds. Anybody who wants to stay here now really wants to stay and the ones who are leaving are going to leave fast, which is a good thing from Dermod's point of view . . ."

Dermod was the fleet commander.

". . . Now make your mind a blank," he ended sourly, "or at least make it blanker than usual."

Conway did not have to try to make his mind a blank, a process which aided the reception of an alien physiology tape. O'Mara's couch was wonderfully soft and comfortable. He had never appreciated it properly before, he seemed to be sinking right into it . . .

A sharp tap on the shoulder made him jump. O'Mara said caustically, "Don't go to sleep! And when you finish with your patient go to bed. Mannen can handle things in Reception and the hospital won't go to pieces without you unless we get hit with an atomic bomb . . ."

With the first evidence of double-mindedness already becoming apparent, Conway left the office. Basically the tape was a brain recording of one of the great medical minds of the species of the patient to be treated. But the doctor taking such a tape had, literally, to share his mind with a completely alien personality. That was how it felt, because *all* the memories and experience of the being who had donated the tape were impressed on the receiving mind, not just selected pieces of medical data. Physiology tapes could not be edited.

But the DBLFs were not as alien as some of the beings Conway had had to share his mind with. Although physically they resembled giant, silvery caterpillars they had a lot in common with Earth-humans. Their emotional reactions to such stimuli as music, a piece of scenic grandeur, or DBLFs of the opposite sex were very nearly identical. This one even liked meat, so that Conway would not have to starve on salad if he had to keep the tape for any length of time.

99

What matter if he *did* feel unsafe walking on just two legs, or found himself humping his back rhythmically as he walked. Or even, when he reached the abandoned DBLF section and the small theatre where the patient had been brought, that a part of his mind thought of Murchison as just another one of those spindly DBDGs from Earth...

Although Murchison had everything ready for him, Conway did not start at once. Because of the mind and personality of the great Kelgian doctor sharing his brain he really *felt* for the patient now. He appreciated the seriousness of its condition and knew that there were several hours of delicate, exacting work ahead of him. At the same time he knew that he was very tired, that he could barely keep his eyes open. It was an effort even to move his feet, and his fingers, when he was checking over the instruments, felt like thick, tired sausages. He knew that he couldn't work in this condition unless he wanted to kill the patient.

"Fix me a pep-shot, will you please?" he said, biting down on a yawn.

For an instant Murchison looked as if she might give him an argument. Pep shots were frowned on in the hospital— their use was sanctioned only in cases of the gravest emergency, and for very good reasons. But she prepared and injected the shot without saying anything, using a blunt needle and quite unnecessary force to jab it home. Even though half his mind wasn't his own, Conway could see that she was mad at him.

Then suddenly the shot took effect. Except for a slight tingling sensation in his feet and a blotchiness which only Murchison could see in his face Conway felt as clear-eyed, alert and physically refreshed as if he had just come out of a shower after ten hours sleep.

"How's the other one?" he asked suddenly. He had been so tired he had forgotten the Kelgian he had left with Murchison in the lock.

"Artificial respiration brought it round," she replied, then with more enthusiasm, "But it was still in shock. I sent it up to the Tralthan section, they still have a few senior staff there..."

"Good," said Conway warmly. He wanted to say more, to be more personally complimentary, but he knew that there was no time to stand and chat. He ended, "Let's begin, shall we...?"

100

Except for the thin-walled, narrow casing which housed the brain the DBLF species had no boney structure. Their bodies were composed of an outer cylinder of musclature which, in addition to being its primary means of locomotion, served to protect the vital organs within it. To the mind of a being more generously reinforced with bones this protection was far from adequate. Another severe disadvantage in the event of injury was its complex and extremely vulnerable circulatory system; the blood-supply network which had to feed the tremendous bands of muscle encircling its body ran close under the skin. The thick fur of the pelt gave some protection here, but not against chunks of jagged-edged, flying metal. An injury which many other species would consider superficial could cause a DBLF to bleed to death in minutes.

Conway worked slowly and carefully, dissolving away the coagulant so hastily applied by Murchison, repairing or partially replacing damaged major blood vessels and sealing off the minor branches which were too fine for him to do anything else. This part of the operation worried him—not because it endangered the life of the patient but because he knew that the beautiful silvery fur would never grow properly in these areas again, that if it grew at all it would be yellowed and visually repulsive to a male Kelgian. The injured nurse was a remarkably handsome young female and such a disfiguration could be a real tragedy. Conway hoped she wouldn't be too proud to keep the area covered with surrogate fur. Admittedly it did not have the rich, deep lustre of living fur and would be immediately recognisable for what it was, but neither would it be so visually distressing ...

An hour ago this would have been just another caterpillar, Conway thought drily, an 'it' about whom he felt only clinical concern. Now he had reached the stage of worrying about the patient's marriage prospects. A physiology tape certainly made one *feel* for one's e-t patients.

When he had finished Conway called Reception, described the patient's condition and urged that it should be evacuated as quickly as possible. Mannen told him that there was half a dozen small vessels loading at the moment, most of them with provision for taking oxy-breathers, and gave him a choice of two Locks in the vicinity. Mannen added that, with the exception of a few patients on the critically ill list, all patients of classifications A through G had either gone or were on the point of going, along with staff members of the same classifications who had been ordered to go by O'Mara for security reasons.

Some of them had displayed extreme reluctance to leave. One in particular, a hoary old Tralthan Diagnostician who was unfortunate enough to own a personal space yacht—something which in normal conditions would *not* have been considered a misfortune!—had had to be formally charged with attempted treason, disturbing the peace and incitement to mutiny and arrested, that being the only way to get it aboard ship.

As he broke the connection Conway thought that they wouldn't have to go to such lengths to get him to leave the hospital. He shook his head, angry and ashamed of himself, and gave Murchison instructions for transfering the patient to the ship.

The injured Kelgian had to be enclosed in a pressure tent for the initial stage of its trip through the AUGL ward, which was now open to space. There were no water-breathers left in the big tank and no water, there being more urgent things to do than repairing and refilling a section which would very likely never be used again. The sight of the great tank, empty now, with its walls vacuum dry and the lush, under-water vegetation which had been designed to make the ward seem more homelike to its occupants hanging like pieces of brittle, discoloured parchment made Conway feel horribly depressed. The depression remained with him while they negotiated the three empty chlorine levels below it and came to another air-filled section.

Here they had to pause to allow a procession of TLTUs to pass. Conway was glad of the chance to stop for a while because, although the pep-shot had him still feeling full of artificial beans, Murchison was beginning to droop. As soon as their patient was aboard he thought he would order her off to bed.

Seven TLTUs filed slowly past, their protective spheres anchored to stretcher-carriers driven by sweating, tense-faced orderlies. Unlike those of the methane life-forms these spheres did not collect frost. Instead they emitted a high-pitched, shuddering whine as their generators laboured to maintain the internal temperature at a comfortable, for their occupants, five hundred degrees. Each one of them passed in a wave of heat which Conway could feel six yards away.

If another warhead was to strike here and now, and one

of those globes was opened . . . Conway didn't think there was a worse way to die than to have the flesh boiled off his bones in a blast of super-heated steam.

By the time they had handed the patient over to the ship's medical officer at the Lock, Conway was having difficulty focussing his eyes and his legs had a definite rubbery feel to them. Bed was indicated, he thought, or another pepshot. He had just decided on the former course of treatment when he was collared respectfully by a Monitor officer wearing a heavy-duty suit which was still radiating the cold of space.

"The casualties are here, sir," the officer said urgently. "We brought them in on a supply ship because Reception is tied up with the evacuation. We're locked on to the DBLF section, but the place is empty and you're the first doctor I've seen. Will you take care of them?"

Conway almost asked what casualties, but stopped himself in time. There had been an attack, he remembered suddenly, the attack had been beaten off and the ensuing casualties, whether great or small, were obviously of prime concern to this officer. If he had known that Conway had been too busy to think about the battle and its casualties . . .

"Where did you put them?" said Conway.

"They're still in the ship," the officer replied, relaxing slightly. "We thought it better for someone to look at them before they were moved. Some of them . . . I mean . . . Uh, will you follow me, sir?"

There were eighteen of them, the wreckage of men who had been fished out of the wreckage of a ship, whose suits were still cold to the touch. Only their helmets had been taken off, and that had been to ascertain whether or not they still lived. Conway counted three decompressions, the rest being fractures of varying degrees of complication one of which was quite definitely a depressed fracture of the skull. There were no radiation cases. So far it had been a clean war, if any war could have been described as clean . . .

Conway felt himself getting angry, but fought it back. This was no time to become emotional over broken, bleeding and asphysiated patients or the reasons for them being in that condition. Instead he straightened and turned to Murchison.

"I'll take another pep-shot," he said briskly, "this will be a long session. But first I'll have the DBLF tape erased and try to round up some help. While I'm gone you might see to getting these men out of their suits and moved to DBLF theatre Five, then you can catch up on your sleep.

"And thank you," he added awkwardly, not wanting to say too much because the Corpsman was still at his elbow. If he had tried to say the things he wanted to say to Murchison with eighteen urgent cases lying around their feet the officer would have been scandalised, and Conway would not have blamed him. But dammit the Corpsman hadn't been working beside Murchison for the last three hours, with a pep-shot heightening all his senses . . .

"If it would help you," said Murchison suddenly, "I could take a pep-shot, too."

Gratefully, Conway said, "You're a very silly girl, but I was hoping you would say that . . ."

## Chapter Seventeen

By THE eighth day all the extra-terrestrial patients had been evacuated and with them had gone nearly four-fifths of the hospital's staff. On the levels which maintained extremes of temperature, pressure or gravity the power was withdrawn causing the ultra-frigid solids to melt and gasify and the dense or superheated atmospheres to condense into a sludgy liquid mess on the floors. Then as the days passed more and more Corpsmen of the Engineering Division arrived, converting the one-time wards into barracks and tearing out large sections of the outer hull so that they could erect projector bases and launching platforms. Dermod's idea now was that Sector General should defend itself instead of relying completely on the fleet, which had already shown that it wasn't capable of stopping everything. By the twenty-fifth day Sector General had made the transition from being a defenceless hospital into what amounted to a heavily armed military base.

Because of its tremendous size and vast reserves of power —several times greater than that of the mobile forces defending it—the weapons were many and truly formidable. Which was as well because on the twenty-ninth day they were tested to the utmost in the first major attack by the enemy.

It lasted for three days.

Conway knew that there were sound, logical reasons for the Corps fortifying the hospital as they had done, but he didn't like it. Even after that fantastic, three-day long attack when the hospital had been hit four times—again with chemical warheads, luckily—he still felt wrong about it. Every time he thought of the tremendous structure which had been dedicated to the highest ideals of humanity and medicine being made into an engine of destruction, geared to a hellish and unnatural ecology wherein it produced its own casualties, Conway felt angry and sad and not a little sickened by the whole ghastly mess. Sometimes he was apt to give vent to his opinions . . .

It was five weeks after the beginning of the evacuation and he was lunching with Mannen and Prilicla. The main dining hall was no longer crowded at mealtimes and green uniformed Corpsmen heavily outnumbered the e-ts at the tables, but there were still upwards of two hundred extraterrestrials in the place and this was what Conway was currently objecting to.

". . . I still say it's a waste," he said angrily, "a waste of lives, of medical talent, everything! All the cases are, and will continue to be, Monitor casualties. Every one an Earth-human. So there are no juicy e-t cases for them to work on. The e-t staff should be sent home!

"Present company included," he ended, with a glare at Prilicla before he turned to face Mannen.

Dr. Mannen made an incision in his steak and hefted a generous forkful mouthwards. Since the disappearance of all his light-gravity patients he had had his LSVO and MSVK tapes erased and so had no mental restrictions placed on his diet. In the five weeks since the evacuation he had noticeably put on weight.

"To an e-t," he said reasonably, "we *are* juicy e-ts."

"You're quibbling," said Conway. "What I'm objecting to is senseless heroics."

Mannen raised his eye-brows. "But heroics are nearly always senseless," he said drily, "and highly contagious as well. In this case I'd say the Corps started it by wanting to defend this place, and because of that we felt obliged to stay also to look after the wounded. At least a few of us feel like that, or we *think* a few of us feel like that.

"The sane, logical thing to do would have been to get

while the going was good," Mannen continued, not quite looking at Conway, "and not a word would have been said to those who got. But then these sane, logical people have colleagues or, uh, friends who they suspect might be in the true hero category, and they won't leave because of what they imagine their friends will think of them if they run away. So they'd sooner *die* than have their friends think they were cowards, and they stay."

Conway felt his face getting warm, but he didn't say anything.

Mannen grinned suddenly and went on, "But this is a form of heroism, too. A case of Death before Dishonour, you might say. And before you can turn round twice everybody is a hero of one kind or the other. And no doubt the e-ts ..." He gave a sly glance at Prilicla. ". . . are staying for similar reasons. And also, I suspect, because they don't want it thought that Earth-human DBDGs have a monopoly on heroism."

"I see," said Conway. He knew that his face was flaming red. It was now quite obvious that Mannen knew that the only reason he had stayed in the hospital was because Murchison, O'Mara and Mannen himself might have been disappointed in him if he'd left. And at the other side of the table Prilicla, the emotion sensitive, would be reading him like a book. Conway thought that he had never felt worse in his whole life.

"You are so right," said Prilicla suddenly, deftly inserting its fork into the plate of spaghetti before it and using two mandibles to twist. "If it had not been for the heroic example of you DBDGs I would have been on the second ship out."

"The second?" asked Mannen.

"I am not," said Prilicla, waving spaghetti for emphasis, "completely without valour."

Listening to the by-play Conway thought that the honest thing would have been for him to admit his cowardice to them, but he also knew that to do so would be to cause embarrassment all round. It was plain that they both knew him for the coward he was and were telling him in their separate fashions that it didn't matter. And looking at it objectively it really did not matter, because there would be no more ships leaving Sector General and its remaining staff were going to be heroes whether they liked it or not. But

Conway still did not think it right that he should be given credit for being a brave, selfless, dedicated man of medicine when he was nothing of the sort.

Before he could say anything, however, Mannen switched subjects abruptly. He wanted to know where Conway and Murchison had been during the fourth, fifth and sixth days of the evacuation. He said that it was highly suggestive that both of them were out of circulation at exactly the same time and he began to list some of the suggestions which occurred to him—which were colourful, startling and next to physically impossible. Soon Prilicla joined in, although the sexual mores of two Earth-human DBDGs could have at most only an academic interest to a sexless GLNO, and Conway was defending himself strenuously from both sides.

Both Prilicla and Mannen knew that Murchison and himself, along with about forty other members of the staff, had been keeping at peak operating efficiency by means of pep-shots for nearly sixty hours. Pep shots did not give something for nothing, and Conway and the others had been forced to adopt the horizontal position of the patient for three days while they recovered from an advanced state of exhaustion. Some of them had literally dropped in their tracks and been taken away hurriedly, so exhausted that the involuntary muscles of heart and lungs were threatening to give up with everything else. They had been taken to special wards where robot devices massaged their hearts, gave artificial respiration and fed them intraveneously.

Still, it *did* look bad that Conway and Murchison had not been seen around together, or separately, or *at all* for three whole days . . .

The alarm siren saved Conway just as the counsels for the prosecution were having it all their own way. He swung out of his seat and sprinted for the door with Mannen pounding along behind him and Prilicla, its not quite atrophied wings aided by its anti-gravity devices, whirring away in front.

Come Hell, high water or interstellar war, Conway thought warmly as he headed for his wards, while there was a reputation to blacken or a leg to pull, Mannen would be there with the latest scandal and prepared to exert traction on the limb in question until it threatened to come off at the acetabulum. In the circumstance all this scandal-mongering had irritated Conway at first, but then he had begun to realise that Mannen was making him see that the whole word hadn't

107

come to an end yet, that this was still Sector General—a frame of mind rather than a place—and that it would continue to be Sector General until the last one of its dedicated and often wacky staff had gone.

When he reached his ward the siren, a constant reminder of the probable manner of their going, had stopped.

Pressure tents hung slackly over all twenty-eight occupied beds, already sealed and with their self-contained air units operating against the possibility of the ward being opened suddenly to space. The nurses on duty, a Tralthan, a Nidian and four Earth-humans, were struggling into their suits. Conway did the same, sealing everything as the others had done with the exception of the faceplate. He made a quick round of his patients, expressed approval to the Tralthan Senior Nurse, then opened the switch which cut off the artificial gravity grids in the floor.

Irregularities in the power supply, and that was no rare occurrence when the hospital's defensive screens were under attack or its weapons went into action, could cause the artificial gravity grid to vacillate between one half and two Gs, which was not a good thing when the patients were mainly fracture cases. It was better to have no gravity at all.

Once patients and staff were protected so far as was possible there was nothing to do but wait. To keep his mind off what was going on outside Conway insinuated himself into an argument between a Tralthan nurse and one of the red-furred Nidians about the modifications currently going on in the giant Translator computor. This vast electronic brain—the Translator packs which everyone wore were merely extensions of it, just sending and receiving units—which handled all the e-t translations in the hospital was, since the evacuation, operating at only a small fraction of its full potential. Hearing this Dermod, the fleet commander, had ordered the unused sections to be re-programmed to deal with tactical and supply problems. But despite the Corps' reassurances that they were allowing ample circuits for Translation the two nurses were not quite happy. Suppose, they said, there should be an occasion when all the e-ts were talking at once?

Conway wanted to tell them that in his opinion the e-ts, especially the nurses, were always talking period so that there was really no problem, but he couldn't think of a tactful way of phrasing it.

An hour passed without anything happening so far as the

hospital was concerned; no hits and no indication that its massive armament had been used. The nurses on duty were relieved by the next shift, three Tralthans and three Earth-humans this time, the senior nurse being Murchison. Conway was just settling down to a very pleasant chat when the siren sounded a steady, low-pitched, faintly derisive note. The attack was over.

Conway was helping Murchison out of her suit when the PA hummed into life.

"Attention, please," it said urgently. "Will Doctor Conway go to Lock Five at once, please . . ."

*Probably a casualty,* Conway thought, *one they are not sure how to move* . . . But then the PA shifted without a break into another message.

". . . Will Doctor Mannen and Major O'Mara go to Lock Five immediately, please . . ."

What, Conway wondered, could be at Lock Five which required the services of two Senior Physicians and the Chief Psychologist. He began to hurry.

O'Mara and Mannen had been closer to Five to begin with and so were there ahead of him by a few seconds. There was a third person in the lock antechamber, clad in a heavy-duty suit with its helmet thrown back. The newcomer was greying, had a thin, lined face and a mouth which was like a tired grey line, but the overall harshness was offset by a pair of the softest brown eyes Conway had ever seen in a man. The insignia on his collar was more ornate than Conway had ever seen before, the highest ranking Corps officer he'd had dealings with being a Colonel, but he knew instinctively that this was Dermod, the fleet commander.

O'Mara tore off a salute which was returned as punctiliously as it had been given, and Mannen and Conway received handshakes with apologies for the gauntlets being worn. Then Dermod got straight down to business.

"I am not a believer in secrecy when it serves no useful purpose," he began crisply. "You people have elected to stay here to look after our casualties, so you have a right to know what is happening whether the news is good or bad. Being the senior Earth-human medical staff remaining in the hospital, and having an understanding of the probable behaviour of your staff in various contingencies, I must leave it up to you whether this information should or should not be made public."

He had been looking at O'Mara. His eyes moved quickly to Mannen, then Conway, then back to O'Mara again. He went on, "There has been an attack, a completely surprising attack in that it was totally abortive. We did not lose a single man and the enemy force was completely wiped out. They didn't seem to know the first thing about deployment or ... or anything. We were expecting the usual sort of attack, vicious, pressed home regardless of cost, that previously has taken everything we've got to counter. This was a massacre ..."

Dermod's voice and the look in his eyes, Conway noted, did not reflect any joy at the victory.

"... Because of this we were able to investigate the enemy wreckage quickly enough to have a chance of finding survivors. Usually we're too busy licking our own wounds to have time for this. We didn't find any survivors, but ..."

He broke off as two Corpsmen came through the inner seal carrying a covered stretcher. Dermod was looking straight at Conway when he went on.

He said, "You were on Etla, Doctor, and will see the implications behind this. And at the same time you might think about the fact that we are under attack by an enemy who refuses either to communicate or negotiate, fights as though driven by a fanatical hatred, and yet uses only limited warfare against us. But first you'd better take a look at this."

When the cover was pulled off the stretcher nobody said anything for a long time. *It* was the tattered, grisly remnant of a once-living, thinking and feeling entity who was now too badly damaged even to classify with any degree of accuracy. But enough remained to show that *it* was not and never had been a human being.

The war, Conway thought sickly, was spreading.

# *Chapter Eighteen*

SINCE *Vespasian* left Etla we have been trying to infiltrate the Empire with our agents," Dermod resumed quietly, "and have been successful in planting eight groups including one on the Central World itself. Our intelligence regarding public opinion, and through it the propaganda machinery used to guide it, is fairly dependable.

"We know that feeling against us is high over the Etla business," he continued, "or rather what we are supposed to have done to the Etlans, but I'll come to that later. This latest development will make things even worse for us . . ."

According to the Imperial government, Dermod explained, Etla had been invaded by the Monitor Corps. Its natives, under the guise of being offered medical assistance, had been callously used as guinea-pigs to test out various types of bacteriological weapons. As proof of this hadn't the Etlans suffered a series of devastating plagues which had commenced within days of the Monitors leaving? Such callous and inhuman behavior could not go unpunished, and the Emperor was sure that every citizen was behind him in the decision he had taken.

But information received—again according to Imperial sources—from a captured agent of the invaders made it plain that their behaviour on Etla was no isolated instance of wanton brutality. On that luckless planet the invaders had been preceded by an extra-terrestrial—a stupid, harmless being sent to test the planet's defences before landing themselves, a mere tool about which they had denied any connection or knowledge when later they contacted the Etlan authorities. It was now plain that they made wide use of such extra-terrestrial life-forms. That they used them as servants, as experimental animals, probably as food . . .

There was a tremendous structure maintained by the invaders, a combination military base and laboratory, where atrocities similar to those practised on Etla were carried on as a matter of course. The invader agent, who had been tricked into giving the spatial coordinates of this base, had confessed to what went on there. It appeared that the invaders ruled over a large number of differing extra-terrestrial species, and it was here that the methods and weapons were developed which held them in bondage.

The Emperor stated that he was quite willing, indeed he considered it his duty, to use his forces to stamp out this foul tyranny. He also felt that he should use only Imperial forces, because he had to confess with shame that relations between the Empire and the extra-terrestrials within its sphere of influence had not always been as warm as they should

111

have been. But if any of these species who may have been slighted in the past were to offer their aid, he would not refuse it . . .

". . . And this explains many of the puzzling aspects of these enemy attacks," Dermod went on. "They are restricting themselves to vibratory and chemical weapons, and in the confined space of our defence globe we must do the same, because this place must be captured rather than destroyed. The Emperor must find out the positions of the Federation planets to keep the war going. The fact that they fight viciously and to the death can be explained by their being afraid of capture, because to them the hospital is nothing but a spacegoing torture chamber.

"And the completely ineffectual recent attack," he continued, "must have been mounted by some of the hot-headed e-t friends of the Empire, who were probably allowed to come here without proper training or information about our defences. They were wiped out, and *that* will cause a lot of e-ts on their side who are wavering to make up their minds.

"In the Empire's favour," he ended bitterly.

When the fleet commander stopped speaking Conway remained silent; he had had access to the Empire reports sent to Williamson and knew that Dermod was not exaggerating the situation. O'Mara had had similar information and maintained the same grim silence. But Dr. Mannen was not the silent type.

"But this is ridiculous!" he burst out. "They're twisting things! This is a hospital, not a torture chamber. And they're accusing us of the things they are doing themselves . . . !"

Dermod ignored the outburst, but in such a way as not to give offence. He said soberly, "The Empire is unstable politically. With enough time we could replace their present government with something more desirable. The Imperial citizens would do it themselves, in fact. But we need time. And we also have to stop the war from spreading too much, from gaining too much momentum. If too many extra-terrestrial allies join the Empire against us the situation will become too complex to control, the original reasons for fighting, or the truth or otherwise of these accusations, will cease to matter.

"We can gain time by holding out here as long as possible," he ended grimly, "but there isn't much we can do about restricting the war. Except hope."

He swung his helmet forward and began to fasten it, although his face-plate was still open for conversation. It was then that Mannen asked the question which Conway had wanted to ask for a long time, but fear of being thought a coward had stopped him from asking it.

"Do we have any chance, really, of holding out?"

Dermod hesitated a moment, obviously wondering whether to be reassuring or to tell the truth. Then he said, "A well-supported and supplied defensive globe is the ideal tactical position. It can also, if the enemy outnumbers it sufficiently, be a perfect trap ..."

When Dermod left, the specimen he had brought with him was claimed by Thornnastor, the Tralthan Diagnostician-in-Charge of Pathology, who would no doubt be happy with it for days. O'Mara went back to bullying his charges into remaining sane, and Mannen and Conway went back to their wards. The reaction of the staff to the possibility of e-ts attacking them was about equally divided between concern over the war spreading and interest regarding the possible methods necessary to treat casualties belonging to a brand new species.

But two weeks passed without the expected attack developing. The Monitor Corps warships continued to arrive, shoot their astrogators back in life-ships, and take up their positions. From the hospital's direct vision ports they seemed to cover the sky, as if Sector General was the centre of a vast, tenuous star cluster with every star a warship. It was an awesome and tremendously reassuring sight, and Conway tried to visit one of the direct vision panels at least once every day.

Then on the way back from one of these visits he ran across a party of Kelgians.

For a moment he couldn't believe his eyes. *All* the Kelgian DBLFs had been evacuated, he had watched the last of them go himself, yet here were twenty-odd of the outsize caterpillars humping along in single file. A closer look showed that they were not wearing the usual brassard with engineering or medical emblems on it—instead their silvery fur was dyed with circular and diamond patterns of red, blue and black. This was Kelgian military insignia. Conway went storming off to O'Mara.

"... I was about to ask the same question, Doctor," the Chief Psychologist said gruffly, indicating his vision screen, "although in much more respectful language. I'm trying to

113

get the fleet commander now, so stop shouting and sit down!"

Dermod's face appeared a few minutes later. His tone was polite but hurried when he said, "This is not the Empire, gentlemen. We are obliged to inform the Federation government and through it the people of the true state of affairs as we see them, although the item about our being attacked by an enemy e-t force has not yet been made public.

"But you must give the e-ts within the Federation credit for having the same feelings as ourselves," he went on, "Extra-terrestrials have stayed behind at Sector General, and on their various home worlds their friends are beginning to feel that they should come out here and help defend them. It is as simple as that."

"But you said that you didn't want the war to spread," Conway protested.

"I didn't ask them to come here, Doctor," Dermod said sharply, "but now they're here I can certainly use them. The latest intelligence reports indicate that the next attack may be decisive . . ."

Later over lunch Mannen received the news about the e-t defenders with the deepest gloom. He was beginning to enjoy being only himself and guzzling steak at dinner, he told Conway sadly, and now with the likelihood of e-t casualties coming in it looked as if they were all going to be tape-ridden again. Prilicla ate spaghetti and observed how lucky it was that the e-t staff hadn't left the hospital after all, not looking at Conway when it said it, and Conway said very little.

*The next attack,* Dermod had said, *may be decisive . . .*

It began three weeks later after a period during which nothing happened other than the arrival of a volunteer force of Tralthans and a single ship whose crew and planet of origin Conway had never heard of before, and whose classification was QLCL. He learned that Sector General had never had the opportunity of meeting these beings professionally because they were recent, and very enthusiastic, members of the Federation. Conway prepared a small ward to receive possible casualties from this race, filling it with the horribly corrosive fog they used for an atmosphere and stepping up the lighting to the harsh, actinic blue which QLCLs considered restful.

The attack began in an almost leisurely fashion. Conway thought as he watched it through the observation panel. The main defense globe seemed barely disturbed by the three minor attacks launched at widely separate points on its surface. All that was visible was three tiny, confused swirls of activity—moving points of light that were ships, missiles, counter-missiles and explosions—which looked too slow to be dangerous. But the slowness was only apparent, because the ships were manoeuvring at a minimum of five Gs, with automatic anti-gravity devices keeping their crews from being pulped by the tremendous accelerations in use, and the missiles were moving at anything up to fifty Gs. The wide-flung repulsion screens which sometimes deflected the missiles were invisible as were the pressors and rattlers which nearly always stopped those which the screens missed. Even so this was merely an initial probing at the hospital's defences, a series of offensive patrols, the curtain-raiser . . .

Conway turned away from the view-port and began moving towards his post. Even the unimportant skirmishes produced casualties and he really had no business being up here sight-seeing. Besides, he would get a much truer picture of how the battle was going down in the wards.

For the next twelve hours casualties arrived in a steady trickle, then the light, probing attacks changed to heavy, feinting thrusts and the wounded came in an irregular stream. Then the attack proper began and they became a flood.

He lost all sense of time, of who his assistants were, of the number of cases he dealt with. There were many times when he needed a pep-shot to clear the fatigue from his mind and hands, but pep-shots were now forbidden regardless of circumstances—the medical staff were hard-pressed enough without some of them becoming patients. Instead he had to work tired, knowing that he was not bringing everything he had to the treatment of his patients, and he ate and slept when he reached the point of not being able to hold his instruments properly. Sometimes it was the towering bulk of a Tralthan at his side, sometimes a Corpsman medical orderly, sometimes Murchison. *Mostly* it was Murchison, he thought. Either she didn't need to sleep, or she snatched a catnap the same times as he did, or even at a time like this he was more inclined to notice her. It was usually Murchison who pushed food at his unresisting face and told him when he really ought to lie down.

By the fourth day the attack showed no signs of diminishing. The rattlers on the outer hull were going almost constantly, their power drain making the lights flicker.

The principle which furnished artificial gravity for the floor

115

and compensated for the killing accelerations used by the ships also lay behind the weapons of both sides—the repulsion screen, originally a meteor protection device, the tractor and pressor beams, and the rattler which was a combination of both. The rattler pushed and pulled—vibrated—depending on how narrowly it was focused, at up to eighty Gs. A push of eighty Gravities then a pull of eighty gravities, several times a minute. Naturally it was not always focused accurately on target, both ships were moving and taking counter-measures, but it was still tight enough to tear the plating off a hull or, in the case of a small ship, to shake it until the men inside rattled.

There was a lot of rattler work going on now. The Empire forces were attacking savagely, compressing the Monitor defence globe down against the hospital's outer hull. The in-fighting which was taking place was with rattler only, space being too congested to fling missiles about indiscriminately. This applied only to the warring ships, however—there were still missiles being directed at the hospital, probably hundreds of them, and some of them were getting through. At least five times Conway felt the tell-tale shock against the soles of his shoes where his feet were strapped to the operating room floor.

There was no fine diagnostic skill required in the treatment of these rattled men. It was all too plain that they suffered from multiple and complicated fractures, some of them of nearly every bone in their bodies. Many times when he had to cut one of the smashed bodies out of its suit Conway want-ed to yell at the men who had brought it in, "What do you expect me to do with *this* . . . ?"

But *this* was alive, and as a doctor he was supposed to do everything possible to make it stay that way.

He had just finished a particularly bad one, with both Mur-chison and a Tralthan nurse assisting, when Conway became aware of a DBLF in the room. Conway had become familiar with the dyed patterns of colour used by the Kelgian military to denote rank, and he saw that this one bore an additional symbol which identified it as a doctor.

"I am to relieve you, Doctor," the DBLF said in a flat, Translated, hurried voice. "I am experienced in treating be-ings of your species. Major O'Mara wants you to go to Lock Twelve at once."

Conway quickly introduced Murchison and the Tralthan—

116

there was another casualty being floated in and they would be working on it within minutes—then said, "Why?"

"Doctor Thornnastor was disabled when the last missile hit us," the Kelgian replied, spraying its manipulators with the plastic its race used instead of gloves. "Someone with e-t experience is required to take over Thornnastor's patients and the FGLIs which are coming in now at Lock Twelve. Major O'Mara suggests you look at them as soon as possible to see what tapes you need.

"And take a suit, Doctor," the DBLF added as Conway turned to go. "The level above this one is losing pressure . . ."

There had been little for Pathology to do since the evacuation, Conway thought as he propelled himself along the corridors leading to Twelve, but the Diagnostician in charge of that department had demonstrated its versatility by taking over the largest casualty section. In addition to FGLIs of its own species Thornnastor had taken DBLFs and Earth-humans, and the patients who had that lumbering, irascible, incredibly brilliant Tralthan to care for them were lucky indeed. Conway wondered how badly it was injured, the Kelgian doctor hadn't been able to tell him.

He passed a view-port and took a quick look outside. It reminded him of a cloud of angry fireflies. The stanchion he was gripping slapped his hand, telling him that another missile had struck not too far away.

There were two Tralthans, a Nidian and a space-suited QCQL in the antechamber when he arrived as well as the ever present Corpsmen. The Nidian explained that a Tralthan ship had been nearly pulled apart by enemy rattlers but that many of its crew had survived. The tractor beams mounted on Sector General itself had whisked the damaged vessel down to the lock and . . .

The Nidian began to bark at him.

"Stop that!" said Conway irritably.

The Nidian looked startled, then it started to bark again. A few seconds later the Tralthan nurses came over and began to deafen him with their modulated fog-horn blasts, and the QCQL was whistling at him through its suit radio. The Corpsmen, engrossed in bringing the casualties through the boarding tube, were merely looking puzzled. Suddenly Conway began to sweat.

They had been hit again, but because he had not been holding onto anything he had not felt it—but he knew exactly where they had been hit. Conway fumbled with his Translator, rapped it sharply with his knuckles—a completely futile gesture—and kicked himself towards the intercom.

On every circuit he tried things howled and trumpeted and moaned and made gutteral barking sounds, a mad cacaphony that set Conway's teeth on edge. A picture of the theatre he had just left flashed before his mind, with Murchison and the Tralthan and the Kelgian doctor working on that casualty *and not one of them knowing what the other was saying.* Instructions, vital directions, demands for instruments or information on the patient's condition—all would be given in an alien gabble incomprehensible to the theatre staff. He was seeing the picture repeated all over the hospital. Only beings of the same species could make themselves understood to each other, and even that did not hold true in every case. There were Earth-humans who did not speak Universal, who spoke languages native to areas on their home planets and who had to rely on Translators even when speaking to other Earth-humans . . .

From the alien babel Conway's straining ears were able to isolate words and a voice which he could understand. It was intelligence battling through a high level of background noise, and all at once his ears seemed to tune out the static and hear only the voice, the voice which was saying, ". . . Three torps playing follow-my-leader, sir. They blasted a way right through. We *can't* jury-rig a Translator, there's nothing of it left to do it with. The last torp went off inside the computer-room . . ."

Outside the intercom niche the e-t nurses were whistling and growling and moaning at him and at each other. He should be giving instructions for the preliminary examination of his casualties, arranging for ward accommodation, checking on the readiness of the FGLI theatre. But he could not do any of these things because his nursing staff would not understand a word he said.

## Chapter Nineteen

FOR A long time, although it might have only been a few seconds, Conway could not bring himself to leave the alcove which contained the intercom unit, and the Chief Psychologist would have been clinically concerned about the thoughts which were going through his mind just then. But slowly he fought down the panic that made him want to run away and hide somewhere, by reminding himself savagely that there was nowhere to run to and by forcing himself to look at the FGLIs drifting about in the antechamber. The place was literally filled with them.

Conway himself knew only the rudiments of Tralthan physiology, but that was the least of his worries because he could easily take an FGLI tape. What he had to do was to start things moving for them *now*. But it was hard to think of each other and the Corpsmen shouting to know what was the matter and the casualties, many of whom were conscious, making pitiful, frantic noises that were muffled only slightly by their pressure envelopes.

"Sergeant!" Conway bawled suddenly at the senior orderly, waving at the casualties. "Ward Four-B, Two-Hundred and Seventh level. Know where it is?"

The NCO bobbed his head, and Conway turned to the nurses.

He got nowhere with the Nidian and QCQL despite all his efforts at sign language, and it was only when he wrapped his legs around one of the FGLI's fore-limbs and by brute force twisted the appendage containing its visual equipment until the cluster of eyes pointed at where the casualties were going that he got anywhere at all. Finally he made the Tralthans understand—he hoped—that they were to accompany the injured and do what they could for them when they arrived.

Four-B had been given over almost entirely to FGLI casualties and most of the staff were Tralthan also, which meant that some of the patients could be reassured by nurses speaking their own language. Conway refused to think of the other casualties who did not have this advantage. He had been assigned Thornnastor's wards. One thing at a time.

When he reached O'Mara's office the Major wasn't there. Carrington, one of his assistants, explained that O'Mara was busy trying to match up patients and staff into species wherever possible, and that he wanted to see Conway immediately the Doctor was finished in the Tralthan wards. Carrington added that as communications were either dead or tied up with e-ts yelling gibberish at each other would he mind either reporting back here or remaining where he was so

119

that the Major could find him. Ten minutes later Conway had the tape he wanted and was on his way to Four-B.

He had taken FGLI tapes before and they weren't too bad. There was a tendency for him to feel awkward at having to walk on only two feet instead of six, and he wanted to move his head and neck about to follow moving objects instead of merely swivelling his eyes. But it was not until he reached the ward that he realised how fully his Tralthan mind partner had settled in. The rows of Tralthan patients became his most immediate and pressing concern, while only a small part of his mind was engaged with the problem of the Tralthan nurses who were obviously close to panic and whose words, for some odd reason, he could not understand. For the Earth-human nurses—puny, shapeless and unlovely bags of dough—he felt only impatience.

Conway went over to the group of shapeless and unlovely bags, although to the human portion of his mind a couple of them looked very shapely indeed, and said, "Give me your attention, please. I have a Tralthan tape which will enable me to treat these FGLIs, but the Translator breakdown means I can't talk to them or the Tralthan staff. You girls will have to help with the preliminary examinations and in the theatre."

They were all staring at him and losing their fear at being told what to do again by someone in authority, even though they were being told to do the impossible. There were forty-seven FGLI patients in the ward, which included eight new arrivals needing immediate attention. There were only three Earth-human nurses.

"The FGLI staff and yourselves can't talk now," he went on after a moment's hesitation, "but you use the same system of medical notation. Some method of communication can be worked out. It will be slow and roundabout, of course, but you must let them know what we are doing and get their help.

"Wave your arms," he ended, "draw pictures. Above all, use your pretty little heads."

*Soft soap at a time like this*, he thought ashamedly. But it was all he could think of at the moment, he wasn't a psychologist like O'Mara . . .

He had dealt with four of the most urgent cases when Mannen arrived with another FGLI in a stretcher held to the floor with magnets. The patient was Thornnastor and it was

120

immediately obvious that the Diagnostician would be immobilised for a long time to come.

Mannen gave details of Thornnastor's injuries and what he had done about them, then went on, ". . . Seeing that you have the monopoly on Tralthans you'd better handle its post-op nursing. And this is the sanest and quietest ward in the hospital, dammit. What's your secret? Boyish charm, a bright idea, or have you access to a bootleg Translator?"

Conway explained what he was trying to do about the mixed species nurses.

"Ordinarily I don't hold with nurses and doctors passing notes during an op," Mannen said. His face was grey with fatigue, his attempt at humour little more than a conditioned reflex. "But it seemed to work for you. I'll pass the idea on."

They manoeuvred Thornnastor's vast body into one of the padded frameworks used as beds for FGLIs in weightless conditions, then Mannen said, "I've got an FGLI tape, too. Needed it for Thorny, here. Now I've got two QCQLs lined up. Didn't know there was any such beastie until today, but O'Mara has the tape. It's a suit job, that gunk they breath would kill anything that walks, crawls or flies, excluding them. They're both conscious, too, and I can't talk to them. I can see I'm going to have fun."

Suddenly his shoulders drooped and the muscles holding up the corners of his mouth gave up the fight. He said dully, "I wish you'd think of something, Conway. In wards like this where the patients and some nurses are of the same classification it isn't too bad. Relatively, that is. But other places where the casualties and staff are completely mixed, and where singletons among the e-t staff have become casualties in the bombardment, things are rough."

Conway had heard the bombardment, a continuous and irregular series of crashes that had been transmitted through the metal of the hospital as if someone was beating on a discordant gong. He had heard them and tried not to think about them, for he knew that the staff were becoming casualties and the casualties that the staff had been taking care of were becoming casualties twice over.

"I can imagine," Conway said grimly. "But with Thornnastor's wards to look after I've plenty to do—"

"Everybody has plenty to do!" Mannen said sharply, "but someone will have to come up with something quick!"

*What do you want me to do about it?* Conway thought

121

angrily at Mannen's receding back, then he turned to his next patient.

For the past few hours something distinctly odd had been happening in Conway's mind. It had begun with an increasingly strong feeling that he almost knew what the Tralthan nurses in the ward were saying. This he put down to the fact that the FGLI tape he had taken—the complete memory record of an eminent physiologist of that race—had given him a lot of data on Tralthan attitudes and expressions and tones of voice. He had never noticed the effect before—probably, he supposed, because he had never had to deal with so many Tralthans in so short a time before, and he had always had a Translator anyway. But working with mainly Tralthan patients had caused the FGLI recorded personality to gain greater than usual prominence at the expense of the human personality.

There was no struggle for possession of his mind, no conflict in the process. It happened naturally because he was being forced to do so much FGLI type thinking. When he did have occasion to speak to an Earth-human nurse or patient, he had to concentrate hard if the first few words they spoke were not to sound like gibberish to him.

And now he was beginning to hear and understand Tralthan talking.

It was far from perfect, of course. For one thing the elephantine hootings and trumpetings were being filtered through human rather than Tralthan ears to the FGLI within his mind, and suffered distortion and change of pitch accordingly. The words tended to be muffled and growly, but he did get some of them, which meant that he possessed a Translator of sorts. It was a strictly one-way affair, of course. Or was it?

When he was preparing the next case for the theatre he decided to try talking back.

His FGLI alter ego knew how the words should sound, he knew how to work his own vocal cords, and the Earth-human voice was reputed to be one of the most versatile instruments in the Galaxy. Conway took a deep breath and gave forth.

The first attempt was disastrous. It ended in an uncontrollable fit of coughing on his part and spread alarm and consternation for the length and breadth of the ward. But with the third attempt he got through—one of the Tralthan

122

nurses answered him! After that it was just a matter of time until he had enough of the more important directions off pat, and subsequent operations proceeded more quickly, efficiently and with enormously increased chances for the patient.

The Earth-human nurses wre greatly impressed by the odd noises issuing from Conway's overworked throat. At the same time they seemed to see an element of humour in the situation . . .

"Well, well," said a familiar, irascible voice behind him, "a ward full of happy, smiling patients, with the Good Doctor keeping up morale by doing animal impressions. What the blazes do you think you're doing?"

O'Mara, Conway saw with a shock, was really angry— not just playing his usual, short-tempered self. In the circumstances it would be better to answer the question and ignore the rhetoric.

"I'm looking after Thornnastor's patients, plus some new arrivals," Conway said quietly. "The Corpsmen and FGLI patients have been taken care of, and I was about to ask you for a DBLF tape for the Kelgians who have just come in."

O'Mara snorted. "I'll send down a Kelgian doctor to take care of that," he said angrily, "and your nurses can take care of the others for the time being. You don't seem to realise that this is one level out of three-hundred eighty-four, Doctor Conway. That there are ward patients urgently in need of the simplest treatment or medication, and they won't get it because the staff concerned whistle while they cheep. That the casualties are piling up around the locks, some of them in corridors which have been opened to space. Those pressure littlers won't supply air forever, you know, and the people in them can't be feeling very happy . . ."

"What do you want me to do?" said Conway.

For some reason this made O'Mara angrier. He said bitingly, "I don't know, Doctor Conway. I am a psychologist. I can no longer act effectively because most of my patients no longer speak the same language. Those who do I've tried to chivvy into thinking of something to get us out of this mess. But they're all too busy treating the sick in their own neighbourhood to think of the hospital as a whole. They want to leave it to the Big Brains . . ."

"In these circumstances," Conway put in, "a Diagnostician

seems to be the logical person to come up with a bright idea."

O'Mara's anger was being explained, Conway thought. It must be pretty frustrating for a psychologist who could neither listen or talk to his patients. But the anger seemed almost personal, as if Conway himself had fallen down on the job in some fashion.

"Thornnastor is out of the picture," O'Mara said, lowering his voice slightly. "You were probably too busy to know that the other two Diagnosticians who stayed behind were killed earlier today. Among the Senior Physicians, Harkness, Irkultis, Mannen—"

"Mannen! Is he . . . ?"

"I thought you might have known about him," O'Mara said almost gently, "since it happened just two levels away. He was working on two QCQLs when the theatre was opened up. A piece of flying metal ruptured his suit. He's decompressed, and before that poison they use for air escaped completely he breathed some of it. But he'll live."

Conway found that he had been holding his breath. He said, "I'm glad."

"Me, too," said O'Mara gruffly. "But what I started to say was that there are no Diagnosticians left and no Senior Physicians other than yourself, and the place is in a mess. As the senior surviving medical officer in the hospital, what do you plan to do about it?"

He stood watching Conway, and waiting.

# Chapter Twenty

CONWAY HAD thought that nothing could make him feel worse than the realisation some hours previously that the Translator system had broken down. He didn't want this responsibility, the very thought of it scared him to death. Yet there had been times when he'd dreamed of being Sector General's director and having absolute control over all things medical within the gigantic organisation. But in those dreams the hospital had not been a dying, war-torn behemoth that was virtually paralysed by the breakdown of communications between its seperate and vital organs, nor had it bristled with death-dealing weapons, nor had it been criminally understaffed and horribly overcrowded with patients.

Probably these were the only circumstances which would allow someone like himself to become Director of a hospital like this, Conway told himself sadly. He wasn't the best available, he was the only one available. Even so it gave him a quite indescribable feeling, compounded of fear, anger and pride, that he was to be its head for the remaining days or weeks of its life.

Conway gave a quick look around his ward, at the orderly if uneven rows of Tralthan and Earth-human beds and at the quietly efficient staff. He had made it this way. But he was beginning to see that he had been hiding himself down here, that he had been running away from his responsibilities.

"I do have an idea," he said suddenly to O'Mara. "It isn't a good idea, and I think we ought to go to your office to talk about it, because you'll probably object to it, loudly, and that might disturb the patients."

O'Mara looked at him sharply. When he spoke the anger had gone from his voice so that it was merely normally sarcastic again. He said, "I find *all* your ideas objectionable, Doctor. It's because I've got such an orderly mind."

On the way to O'Mara's office they passed a group of high-ranking Monitor officers and the Major told him that they were part of Dermod's staff who were preparing to shift tactical command into the hospital. At the moment Dermod was commanding from *Vespasian*. But even the capital ships were taking a beating now, and the fleet commander had already had *Domitian* not quite shot from under him . . .

When they arrived Conway said, "It isn't such a hot idea, and seeing those Corpsmen on the way up here has given me a better one. Suppose we ask Dermod to let us use his ship Translators . . . ?"

O'Mara shook his head. "It won't work," he said. "I thought of that idea, too. It seems the only Translator computers of any use to us are on the big ships, and they are such an integral part of the structure that it would practically wreck the ship to take one out. Besides, for our absolute minimum needs we would require twenty capital ship computers. We haven't got twenty capital ships left, and what we do have Dermod says he has a much better use for. "Now what was your other not very good idea?"

Conway told him.

When he had finished, O'Mara looked at him steadily for nearly a minute. Finally he said, "Consider your idea objected to, but strongly. Consider, if you like, that I jumped up and down and pounded the desk, because that is what I'd be doing if I wasn't so blasted tired. Don't you realise what you'd be letting yourself in for?"

From somewhere below them came a tearing crash with ridiculous, gong-like overtones. Conway jerked involuntarily, then said, "I think so. There will be a lot of mental confusion and discomfort, but I hope to avoid most of it by letting the tape entity take over almost completely until I have what I need, then I partly suppress it and do the translation. That was how it worked with the Tralthan tape and there's no reason why it shouldn't work with DBLFs or any of the others. The DBLF language should be a cinch, it being easier to moan like a Kelgian than hoot like a Tralthan..."

He would not have to stay in any one place for very long, Conway hoped, only long enough to sort out the local translation problems. Some of the e-t sounds would be difficult to reproduce orally, but he had an idea for modifying certain musical instruments which might take care of that. And he would not be the only walking Translator, there were still e-t and human doctors who could help by taking one or two tapes. Some of them might have done so already, but had not thought of using them for translation yet. As he talked Conway's tongue was having a hard job to keep up with his racing mind.

"Just a minute," said O'Mara at one point. "You keep talking about letting one personality come to the fore, then suppressing it, then bringing out two together and so on. You might find that you haven't that much control. Multiple physiology tapes are tricky, and you've never had more than two before at any one time. I have your records."

O'Mara hesitated for a moment, then went on seriously, "What you get is the recorded memories of an e-t high in the medical profession on its home planet. It *isn't* an alien entity fighting for possession of your mind, but because its memory and personality are impressed alongside your own you may be panicked into thinking that it is trying to take over.

Some of our tapes were taken from very aggressive individuals, you see.

"Odd things happen to doctors who take a number of long-term tapes for the first time," O'Mara went on. "Pains, skin conditions, perhaps organic malfunctionings develop. All have a psychosomatic basis, of course, but to the person concerned they hurt just as much as the real thing. These disturbances can be controlled, even negated, by a strong mind. Yet a mind with strength alone will break under them in time. Flexibility allied with strength is required, also something to act as a mental anchor, something that you must find for yourself . . .

"Suppose I agree to this," he ended abruptly, "how many will you need?"

Conway thought quickly. Tralthan, Kelgian, Melfan, Nidian, the ambulating plants he had met before going to Etla, who also had remained behind, and the beasties Mannen had been treating when he was knocked out of it. He said, "FGLI, DBLF, ELNT, Nidian-DBDG, AACP and QCQL. Six."

O'Mara compressed his lips. "I wouldn't mind if it was a Diagnostician doing this," he objected, "because they are used to splitting their minds six ways. But you are just—"

"The senior medical officer of the hospital," Conway finished for him, grinning.

"Hm," said O'Mara.

In the silence they could hear human voices and a peculiar, alien gabbling go past in the corridor outside. Whoever was making the noise must have been shouting very loud because the Major's office was supposed to be soundproof.

"All right," said O'Mara suddenly, "you can try it. But I don't want to have deal with you in my professional capacity, and that is a much stronger possibility than you seem to think. We're too short of doctors to have you immobilising yourself in a straight-jacket, so I'm going to set a watchdog on you. We'll add GLNO to your list."

"Prilicla!"

"Yes. Being an empath it has had a hard time with the sort of emotional radiation that is going around recently, and I've had to keep it under sedation. But it will be able to keep a mental eye on you, and probably help you, too. Move over to the couch."

Conway moved to the couch and O'Mara fitted the helmet. Then the Major began to talk softly, sometimes asking questions, sometimes just talking. Conway should be unconscious for a multiple transfer, he said, he should in fact sleep for at least four hours for the best results, and he needed sleep anyway. Probably, O'Mara said, he had thought up this whole, harebrained scheme just to have a legitimate excuse to sleep. He had a big job ahead, the psychologist told him quietly, and he would really need to be in seven places as well as being seven people at once, so that a sleep would do him good . . .

"It won't be too bad," Conway said, struggling to keep his eyes open. "I'll stay in any one place only long enough to learn a few basic words and phrases that I can teach to the nursing staff. Just enough so they'll understand when an e-t surgeon says 'Scalpel,' or 'Forceps' or 'Stop breathing down the back of my neck, Nurse . . .' "

The last words that Conway heard clearly were O'Mara saying, "Hang onto your sense of humour, lad. You're going to need it . . ."

He awoke in a room that was too large and too small, alien in six different ways and at the same time completely familiar. He did not feel rested. Clinging to the ceiling by six pipestem legs was a tiny, enormous, fragile, beautiful, disgustingly insectile creature that reminded him of his worst nightmares the amphibious *cllels* he used to hunt at the bottom of his private lake for breakfast, and many other things including a perfectly ordinary GLNO Cinrusskin like himself. It was beginning to quiver slightly in reaction to the emotional radiation he was producing. All of him knew that the GLNOs from Cinruss were empaths.

Fighting his way to the surface of a maelstrom of alien thoughts, memories and impressions Conway decided that it was time to go to work. Prilicla was immediately available for the first test of his idea. He began searching for and bringing up the GLNO memories and experiences, sifting through a welter of alien data for the type of information which is not consciously remembered but is constantly in use —data on the Cinrusskin language.

No, *not* the Cinrusskin language, he reminded himself sharply, *his* language. He had to think and feel and listen like a GLNO. Gradually he began to do it . . .

And it was not pleasant.

128

He was a Cinrusskin, a member of a fragile, low-gravity, insect race of empaths. The handsome, delicately marked exo-skeleton and the youthful, iridescent sheen of Prilicla's not quit atrophied wings were now things which he could properly appreciate, and the way Prilicla's mandibles quivered in sudden concern at his distress. For Conway was a member of an empathic race, all the memories and experience of his GLNO life were those of a normally happy and healthy empath, but now he was an empath no more. He could see Prilicla, but the faculty which let him share the other's emotions, and subtly coloured every word, gesture and expression so that for two Cinrusskins to be within visual range was to be unalloyed pleasure for both, was missing. He could remember having empathetic contact, remember having it all his life, but now he was little more than a deaf mute.

His human brain did not possess the empathetic faculty, and it was not bestowed by filling his mind with memories of having had it.

Prilicla made a series of clicking, buzzing sounds. Conway, who had never spoken with the GLNO other than by means of the toneless and emotion-filtering process of Translation, heard it say "I'm sorry" in a voice full of concern and pity.

In return Conway tried to make the soft trill and click which was Prilicla's name, the true sound of the Earth-human word 'Prilicla' being only a clumsy approximation. On the fifth attempt he succeeded in making something which was close to the sound he wanted.

"That is very good, friend Conway," Prilicla said warmly. "I had not considered this idea of yours possible. Can you understand me?"

Conway sought the word-sounds he needed, then carefully began to form them. "Thank you," he said, "and yes."

They tried more difficult phrases then, technical words to put across obtuse medical and physiological details. Sometimes Conway was able to do it, sometimes not. His was at best only the crudest of pidgin Cinrusskin, but he persevered. Then suddenly there was an interruption.

"O'Mara here," said a voice from his room communicator. "You should be awake now so here is the latest position, Doctor. We are still under attack, but this has eased off somewhat since more volunteer e-ts arrived to reinforce us.

These are Melfans, some more Tralthans and a force of Illensan chlorine-breathers. So you're going to have PVSJs to worry about, too. Then inside the hospital..."

There followed a detailed breakdown of casualties and available staff into species, location and numbers, with further data on problems peculiar to each section and their degree of urgency.

"... It's for you to decide where to start," O'Mara went on, "and the sooner the better. But in case you are still feeling confused I'll repeat—"

"No need," said Conway, "I got it."

"Good. How do you feel?"

"Awful. Horrible. And very peculiar."

"That," said O'Mara drily, "is in all respects a normal reaction. Off."

Conway released the strapping which held him to the bed and swung his legs out. Immediately he stiffened, unable to let go. Many of the beings inhabiting his mind were terrified by weightless conditions and the reaction was instinctive. Because of this it was very difficult to counter, and he had a moment of sheer panic when he discovered that his feet would not stick to the ceiling the way Prilicla's did. And when he did relax his grip on the edge of the bed he found that he had been holding on with an appendage that was pallid and flabby and horribly different to the clean, hard outlines of the mandible he had expected to see. But somehow he managed to cross his room into the corridor and traverse it for a distance of fifty yards.

Then he was stopped.

An irate medical orderly in Corps green wanted to know why he was out of bed and what ward he had come from. The Corpsman's language was colourful and not at all respectful.

Conway became aware then of his large, gross, fragile, loathsome pink body. A perfectly good body, part of his mind insisted, if a little on the skinny side. And this shapeless, puny, monstrosity was encircled, where it was joined by its two lower appendages, by a piece of white fabric which served no apparent purpose. The body looked ridiculous as well as alien.

*Oh damn!* thought Conway, struggling up through a smother of alien impressions, *I forgot to dress.*

# Chapter Twenty-One

CONWAY'S FIRST act was to install one representative from each species in the Communications room. A semblance of order had already been restored to the network by posting Corpsmen at every intercom unit to forbid their use—if the would-be user was not too persistent and well-muscled—to e-ts. This meant that Earth-human personnel could talk to each other. But with e-ts on the switchboard, calls by other species could be answered and redirected. Conway spent nearly two hours, more time than he ever spent anywhere else, putting himself *en rapport* with the e-t operators and devising a list of synonyms which would allow them to pass simple —*very* simple—messages to each other. He had two Monitor language experts with him on it, and it was they who suggested that he made a taped record of this seven-way Rosetta stone, and make others to fit the conditions he would find in the wards.

Wherever he went after that Prilicla, the language experts and a Corps radio technician trailed behind, in addition to the nursing staff he accumulated from time to time. It was an impressive procession, but Conway was in no mood to appreciate it just then.

Earth-human medical staff made up more than half of the present complement, but Earth-human Monitor casualties outnumbered the e-ts by thirty to one. On some levels one nurse had a whole ward of Corpsmen in her charge, with a few Tralthans or Kelgians trying to assist her. In such cases Conway's job was simply that of arranging a minimum of communication between the human and e-t nurses. But there were other instances when the staff were ELNTs and FGLIs and the patients in their charge were DBLF, QCQL and Earth-human, or Earth-humans in charge of ELNTs, or the plant-like AACPs looking after a mixed bag of practically everything. The simple answer would have been to move the patients into the charge of staff of their own species—except that they could not be moved for the reason that they were too ill, that there was no staff available to move them, or that there were no nurses of that particular species. In these cases Conway's job was infinitely more complex.

The shortage of nursing staff of all species was chronic. With regard to doctors the position was desperate. He called O'Mara.

"We haven't enough doctors," he said. "I think nurses should be given more discretion in the diagnosis and treatment of casualties. They should do as they think best without waiting for authority from a doctor who is too busy to supervise anyway. The casualties are still coming in and I can't see any other way of—"

"Do it, you're the boss," O'Mara broke in harshly.

"Right," said Conway, nettled. "Another thing. I've had offers by a lot of the doctors to take two or three tapes for translation purposes in addition to the tape they draw for current ops. And some of the girls have volunteered to do the same—"

"No!" said O'Mara. "I've had some of your volunteers up here and they aren't suitable. The doctors left to us are either very junior interns or Corps medical officers and e-ts who came with the volunteer forces. None of them have experience with multiple physiology tapes. It would render them permanently insane within the first hour.

"As for the girls," he went on, a sardonic edge in his voice, "you have noticed by this time that the female Earth-human DBDG has a rather peculiar mind. One of its peculiarities is a deep, sex-based mental fastidiousness. No matter what they *say* they will not, repeat not, allow alien beings to apparently take over their pretty little brains. If such should happen, severe mental damage would result. No again. Off."

Conway resumed his tour. It was beginning to get him down now. Even though his technique was improving the process of Translation was an increasing strain. And in the relatively easy periods between translations he felt as if there were seven different people all arguing and shouting inside his brain, and his own was very rarely the loudest voice. His throat was raw from making noises that it had never been designed for, and he was hungry.

All seven of him had different ideas for assuaging that hunger, revoltingly different ideas. Since the hospital's catering arrangements had suffered as badly as everything else

132

there was no wide selection from which he could have picked neutral items that would not have offended, or at least not completely nauseated, his alter egos. He was reduced to eating sandwiches with his eyes shut, in case he would find out what was in them, and drinking water and glucose. None of him objected to water.

Eventually an organisation for the reception and treatment of casualties was operating again in all the habitable levels—it was slow, but it was operating. And now that there were facilities for treating them Conway's next job was to move the patients who were currently jamming the approaches to the airlocks. There were actually pressure-litters anchored to the outer hull, he had been told.

Prilicla objected.

For a few minutes he tried to find out why. One of Prilicla's objections was that Conway was tired, which he countered by telling it that everybody in the hospital, including Prilicla itself, was tired. The other objections were either too weak or too subtle for the limited communications available. Conway ignored them and headed for the nearest lock.

The problems here were very similar to those inside the hospital—the major disadvantage being his spacesuit radio which hampered translation considerably. But to offset this he could get around much more quickly. The tractor beam men who handled the wrecks and wreckage around the hospital could whisk his whole party from point to point within seconds.

But he discovered that the Melfan segment of his mind, which had been seriously troubled by the weightless conditions inside the hospital, was utterly terrified outside it. The Melfan ELNT who had produced the tape had been an amphibious, crab-like being who lived mainly under water and had had no experience whatever of space. Conway had to fight down the panic which threatened his whole, multi-tenanted mind as well as the fear which all of him felt at the battle going on above his head.

O'Mara had told him that the attack was easing off, but Conway could not imagine anything more savage than what he was seeing.

Between the warring ships no missiles were being used—the attackers and defenders were too condensed, too inextricably tangled up. Like tiny, fast-moving models, so sharply defined that he felt he could reach up and grab one, the ships wheeled through their wild, chaotic dance. Singly and in groups they lunged, whirled, took frantic evasive action, broke formation or had their formations broken, reformed and attacked again. It was endless, implacable and almost hypnotic. There was, of course, no noise. What missiles were launched were directed at the hospital, a target too big to miss, and they were felt rather than heard.

Between the ships, tractor and pressor beams jabbed out like solid, invisible fingers, slowing or deflecting the target ship so that a rattler could be focussed. Sometimes three or more vessels would converge on a single target and tear it apart within seconds. Sometimes a well-directed rattler would rip apart the artificial gravity system an instant before it disrupted the drive. With the crew hammered flat by high acceleration the ship would go tumbling out of the fight, unless someone put another rattler on it or a tractor man on Sector General's hull pulled it down to look for survivors.

Whether or not there were any survivors the wreck could be used...

The once smooth and shining hull was a mass of deep, jagged-edged craters and buckled plating. And because the missile lightning did strike twice, or even three times, in the same place—that was how the Translator computer had been destroyed—the craters were being plugged with wreckage in an effort to keep the missiles from exploding deeper inside the hospital. Any type of wreckage served, the tractor men weren't choosey.

Conway was on a tractor-beam mount when one of the wrecks was pulled in. He saw the rescue team shooting from the shelter of the airlock, circle the hulk carefully, then enter. About ten minutes later they came out towing... something.

"Doctor," said the NCO in charge of the installation, "I think I goofed. My men say the beastie they've pulled out of that wreck is new to them and want you to have a look. I'm sorry, but one wreck is like any other wreck. I don't think it is one of ours..."

Six parts of Conway's mind contained personalities whose memories did not contain data on the war and they did not think it mattered. As the minority opinion Conway didn't think it mattered either, but he knew that neither the sergeant nor himself had time to start an ethical debate on it.

He had a quick look, then said, "Take it inside. Level Two-forty, Ward Seven."

Since being given the tapes Conway had been forced to watch helplessly while patients—casualties whose condition was such that they merited a fully qualified Senior Physician at least to perform the surgery—were operated on by tired, harassed, but well-intentioned beings who just did not have the required skill. They had done the job as best they could because there was nobody else to do it. Conway had wanted to step in many times, but had reminded himself and been reminded by Prilicla and the rest of his entourage, that he had to consider the Big Picture. Reorganising the hospital then had been more important than any one patient. But now he felt that he could stop being an organiser and go back to being a doctor.

This was a new species to the hospital. O'Mara would not have a tape on its physiology, and even if the patient recovered consciousness it would not be able to cooperate because the Translators were dead. Conway had got to take this one and nobody was going to talk him out of it.

Ward Seven was adjacent to the section where a Kelgian military doctor and Murchison had been working wonders with a mixed bag of FGLI, QCQL and Earth-human patients, so he asked them both to assist. Conway put the new arrival's classification as TRLH, being aided in this by the fact that the patient's spacesuit was transparent as well as flexible. Had the suit been less flexible the being's injuries would have been less severe, but then the suit would have cracked instead of bending with the force which had smashed against it.

Conway bored a tiny hole in the suit, drew off a sample of the internal atmosphere and resealed it. He put the sample in the analyser.

"And I thought the QCQLs were bad," said Murchison when he showed her the result. "But we can reproduce it. You will need to replace the air here, I expect?"

Conway said, "Yes, please."

They climbed into their operating suits—regulation lightweight pattern except that the arms and hands sections ended in a fine, tight-fitting sheath that was like a second skin. The air was replaced by the patient's atmosphere and they began cutting it out of its suit.

The TRLH had a thin carapace which covered its back

135

and curved down and inwards to protect the central area of its underside. Four thick, single-jointed legs projected from the uncovered sections and a large, but again lightly boned head contained four manipulatory appendages, two recessed but extensible eyes and two mouths, one of which had blood coming from it. The being must have been hurled against several metal projections. Its shell was fractured in six places and in one area it had been almost shattered, the pieces being severely depressed. In this area it was losing blood rapidly. Conway began charting the internal damage with the x-ray scanner, then a few minutes later he signalled that he was ready to start.

He wasn't ready, but the patient was bleeding to death.

The internal arrangement of organs was different from anything he had previously encountered, and different from anything in the experience of the six personalities sharing his mind. But from the QCQL he received pointers on the probable metabolism of beings who breathed such highly corrosive air, from the Melfan data on the possible methods of exploring the damaged carapace, and the FGLI, DBLF, GLNO and AACP contributed their experience. But it was not always helpful—at every stage they literally shrieked warnings to be careful, so much so that for seconds at a time Conway stood with his hands shaking, unable to go on. He was probing the recorded memories deeply now, hitherto it had only been for data on language, and *everything* was coming up.

The private nightmares and neuroses of the individuals, triggered off by being so inextricably mixed with the similar alien nightmares around them, and all mounting, growing worse by the minutes. The beings who had produced the tapes did not all have e-t hospital experience, they were not accustomed to alien points of view. The proper thing was to keep reminding himself that they were not separate personalities, Conway told himself, but merely a mass of alien data of different types. But he was horribly, stupidly tired and he was beginning to lose control of what was going on in his mind. And still the memories welled up in a dark, turgid flood. Petty, shameful, secret memories mostly concerned with sex—and that, in e-ts, was *alien*, so alien that he wanted to scream. He found suddenly that he was bent over, sweating, as if there was a heavy weight on his back.

He felt Murchison gripping his arm. "What's wrong, Doctor?" she said urgently. "Can I help?"

He shook his head, because for a second he didn't know how to form words in his own language, but he kept looking at her for all of ten seconds. When he turned back he had a picture of her in his mind as she was to him, not as a Tralthan or a Melfan or a Kelgian saw her. The concern in her eyes had been for him alone. At times Conway had had secret thoughts of his own about Murchison, but they were normal, human thoughts. He hugged them to him tightly and for a time he was in control again. Long enough to finish with the patient.

Then suddenly his mind was tearing itself apart into seven pieces and he was falling into the deepest, darkest pits of seven different Hells. He did not know that his limbs stiffened or bent or twisted as if something alien had separate possession of each one. Or that Murchison dragged him out and held him while Prilicla, at great danger to life and its fragile, spidery limbs, gave him the shot which knocked him out.

## Chapter Twenty-Two

THE INTERCOM buzzer awakened Conway, instantly but without confusion in the pleasant, familiar, cramped surroundings of his own room. He felt rested and alert and ready for breakfast, and the hand he used to push back the sheets had five pink fingers on it and felt just right that way. But then he became aware of a certain strangeness which made him hesitate for a moment. The place was *quiet* . . . !

"To save you the where-am-I-what-time-is-it? routine," O'Mara's voice came wearily, "you have not been consciously with us for two days. During that time, early yesterday, to be exact, the attack ceased and has not yet been resumed and I did a lot of work on you. For your own good you were given a hypno treatment to forget everything, so you will not be eternally grateful for what I've done for you. How do you feel now?"

"Fine," said Conway enthusiastically. "I can't feel any . . .

I mean, there seems to be plenty of *room* in my head . . ."

O'Mara grunted. "The obvious retort is that your head is empty, but I won't make it."

The Chief Psychologist, despite his attempt to maintain his usual dry, sardonic manner, sounded desperately tired—his words were actually slurred with weariness. But O'Mara, Conway knew, was not the type who became tired—he might, if driven long and hard enough, succumb to mental fatigue . . .

"The fleet commander wants a meeting with us in four hours time," O'Mara went on, "so don't get involved with any cases between now and then. Things are running fairly smoothly now, anyway, so you can afford to play hooky for a while. *I'm* going to sleep. Off."

But it was very difficult to spend four hours doing nothing, Conway found. The main dining hall was jammed with Corpsmen—projector crews engaged on hull defence, replacements for the defending ships, maintenancemen and Medical Division personnel who were supplementing the civilian medical staff. Conversation was loud and nervous and too cheerful, and revolved around the past and possible future aspects of the attack.

Apparently the Monitor force had practically been pushed down onto the outer hull when an e-t force of volunteer Illensans had emerged from hyperspace just outside the enemy globe. Illensan ships were big and badly designed and looked like capital ships even though they only had the armament of a light cruiser, and the sight of ten of them popping out of nowhere had put the enemy off his stride. The attacking force had pulled back temporarily to regroup and the Monitors, with nothing to regroup with, were concentrating on increasing the armament of their last line of defence, the hospital itself. But even though it concerned him as closely as anyone else in the room, Conway felt averse to joining in the cheerfully morbid conversations.

Since O'Mara had erased all the physiology tapes and indulged in some curative tinkering with his mind, the nightmare of two days ago and the e-t language data he had gained had faded, so he could not indulge in polite conversation with the e-ts scattered about the hall. And the Earthhuman nurses were being monopolised by Corpsmen, usually at the rate of ten or twelve to one, with an obvious improvement in morale in both directions. Conway ate quickly and left, feeling that his own morale was in need of improvement, too.

Which made him wonder suddenly if Murchison was on duty, off duty or asleep. If she was asleep there was nothing he could do, but if she was on duty he could very soon take her off it, and when she was off...

Strangely he felt only the slightest pricklings of conscience over this shameless abuse of his authority for his own selfish ends. In time of war, he thought, people became less bound by their professional and moral codes. Ethically he was going to the dogs.

But Murchison was just going off duty when he arrived in her ward, so he did not have to openly commit the crime he had been intent on committing. In the same loud, too-cheerful tone that he had considered so artificial when he had heard it in the dining hall he asked if she had any previous engagement, suggested a date, and muttered something horribly banal about all work and no play...

"Previous engage...*play*...! But I want to *sleep*!" she protested; then in more reasonable tones, "You can't...I mean, where would we go, what would we do? The place is a wreck. Would I have to change?"

"The recreation level is still there," Conway said, "and you look fine."

The regulation nurses uniform of blue, tight-fitting tunic and slacks—very tight-fitting so as to ease the problem of climbing in and out of protective suits—flattered Murchison, but she looked worn out. As she unhooked the broad white belt and instrument pouches and removed her cap and hairnet Conway growled deep in his throat, and immediately burst into a fit of coughing because it was still tender from making e-t noises.

Murchison laughed, shaking out her hair and rubbing her cheeks to put some colour into them. She said brightly, "Promise you won't keep me out too late...?"

On the way to the recreation level it was difficult not to talk shop. Many sections of the hospital had lost pressure so that in the habitable levels overcrowding was severe—there was scarcely an air-filled corridor which was not also filled with casualties. And this was a situation which none of them had foreseen. They had not expected the enemy to use limited warfare on them. Had atomic weapons been used there would not have been any overcrowding, or, possibly, any hospital. Most of the time Conway was not listening to Murchison, but she didn't seem to notice. Perhaps because she wasn't listening to him.

The recreation level was the same in detail as they remembered it, but the details had been dramatically changed around. With the hospital's centre of gravity being above the recreation level what little attraction there was was upwards, and all the loose material normally on the ground or in the bay had collected against the roof, where it made a translucent chaos of sand-veined water, air-pockets and trailing watery globes through which the submerged sun shone a deep, rich purple.

"Oh, this is *nice!*" said Murchison. "And restful, sort of."

The lighting gave her skin a warm, dusky coloration that was wholly indescribable, Conway thought, but nice. Her lips —soft purple, verging on black—were parted slightly to reveal teeth which seemed almost iridescent, and her eyes were large and mysterious and glowing.

"The word," he said, "is romantic."

They launched themselves gently into the vast room in the direction of the restaurant. Below them the tree tops drifted past and they ran through a wisp of fog—cooling steam produced by the warm, underwater sun—which beaded their faces and arms with moisture. Conway caught her hand and held it gently, but their velocities were not exactly matching and they began to spin around their centre of gravity. Conway bent his elbow slowly, drawing her towards him, and their rate of spin increased. Then he slid his other arm around her waist and pulled her closer still.

She started to protest and then suddenly, gloriously, she was kissing him and clinging to him as fiercely as he was to her, and the empty bay, cliffs, and purple, watery sky was whirling madly around them.

In a calm, impersonal corner of his mind Conway thought that his head would have been spinning anyway even if his body hadn't, it was that sort of kiss. Then they spun gently into the cliff-top at the other side of the bay and broke apart, laughing.

They used the artificial greenery to pull themselves towards the one-time restaurant. It was dim inside, and during its slow fall ceilingwards a lot of water had collected under the transparent roof and on the undersides of the table canopies. Like some fragile, alien fruit it hung in clusters which stirred gently at their passage or burst into hundreds of tiny silvery globes when they blundered against a table. With the low ceiling and dim light it was difficult to keep from knocking into things and soon the globes were all around them, seeming to crowd in, throwing back a hundred tiny, distorted reflections of Murchison and himself. It was like an alien dream world, Conway thought; and it was a wish-fulfillment dream. The dark, lovely shape of Murchison drifting beside him left no doubt about that.

They sat down at one of the tables, but carefully so as not to dislodge the water in the canopy above them. Conway took her hand in his, the others being needed to hold them onto their chairs, and said, "I want to talk to you."

She smiled, a little warily.

Conway tried to talk. He tried to say the things that he had rehearsed to himself many times, but what came out was a disjointed hodge-podge. She was beautiful, he said, and he didn't want to be friends and she was a stupid little fool for staying behind. He loved her and wanted her and he would have been happy spending months—not too many months, maybe—getting her in a corner where she couldn't say anything but yes. But now there wasn't time to do things properly. He thought about her all the time and even during the TRLH operation it had been thinking about her that let him hang on until the end. And all during the bombardment he had worried in case . . .

"I worried about you, too," Murchison broke in softly. "You were all over the place and every time there was a hit . . . And you always knew exactly what to do and . . . and I was afraid you would get yourself killed."

Her face was shadowed, her uniform clung damply. Conway felt his mouth dry.

She said warmly, "You were wonderful that day with the TRLH. It was like working with a Diagnostician. *Seven* tapes, O'Mara said. I . . . I asked him to give me one, earlier, to help you out. But he said no because . . ." She hesitated, and looked away. ". . . because he said girls are very choosey who they let take possession of them. Their minds, I mean . . ."

"How choosey?" said Conway thickly. "Does the choice exclude . . . friends?"

He leaned forward involuntarily as he spoke, letting go his hold on the chair with his other hand. He drifted heavily up from the table, jarred the canopy and touched one of the

141

floating globes with his forehead. With the surface tension broken it collapsed wetly all over his face. Spluttering he brushed it away, knocking it into a cloud of tiny, glowing marbles. Then he saw it.

It was the only harsh note in this dream world, a pile of unarmed missiles occupying a dark corner of the room. They were held to the floor by clamps and further secured with netting in case the clamps were jarred free by an explosion. There was plenty of slack in the netting. Still holding onto Murchison, he kicked himself over to it, searched until he found the edge of the net, and pulled it up from the floor.

"We can't talk properly if we keep floating into the air," he said quietly. "Come into my parlour . . ."

Maybe the netting was too much like a spider's web, or his tone resembled too closely that of a predatory spider. He felt her hesitate. The hand he was holding was trembling.

"I . . . I know how you feel," she said quickly, not looking at him. "I like you, too. Maybe more than that. But this isn't right. I know we don't have any time, but sneaking down here like this and . . . it's selfish. I keep thinking about all those men in the corridors, and the other casualties still to come. I know it sounds stuffy, but we're supposed to think about other people first. That's why—"

"Thank you," said Conway furiously. "Thank you for reminding me of my duty."

"Oh, please!" she cried, and suddenly she was clinging to him again, her head against his chest. "I don't want to hurt you, or make you hate me. I didn't think the war would be so horrible. I'm frightened. I don't want you to be killed and leave me all alone. Oh, please, hold me tight and . . . and tell me what to do . . ."

Her eyes were glittering and it was not until one of the tiny points of light floated away from them that he realised she was crying silently. He had never imagined Murchison crying, somehow. He held her tightly for a long time, then gently pushed her away from him.

Roughly, he said, "I don't hate you, but I don't want to discuss my exact feelings at the moment, either. Come on, I'll take you home."

But he didn't take her home. The alarm siren went a few minutes later and when it stopped a voice on the PA was asking Doctor Conway to come to the intercom.

142

# Chapter Twenty-Three

ONCE IT had been Reception, with three fast-talking Nidians to handle the sometimes complex problems of getting patients out of their ambulances and into the hospital. Now it was Command Headquarters and twenty Monitor officers murmuring tensely into throat mikes, their eyes glued to screens which showed the enemy at all degrees of magnification from nil to five hundred. Two of the three main screens showed sections of the enemy fleet, the images partly obliterated by the ghostly lines and geometrical figures that was a tactical officer trying to predict what they would do next. The other screen gave a wide-angle view of the outer hull.

A missile came down like a distant shooting star, making a tiny flash and throwing up a minute fountain of wreckage. The tearing, metallic crash which reverberated through the room was out of all proportion to the image.

Dermod said, "They've withdrawn out of range of the heavy stuff mounted on the hospital and are sending in missiles. This is the softening up process designed to wear us down prior to the main attack. A counterattack by our remaining mobile force would result in its destruction, they are so heavily outnumbered that they can operate effectively only if backed by the defences of the hospital. So we have no choice but to soak up this stage as best we can and save our strength for—"

"What strength?" said Conway angrily. Beside him O'Mara made a disapproving noise, and across the desk the fleet commander looked coldly at him. When Dermod spoke it was to Conway, but he didn't answer the question.

"We can also expect small raids by fast, manoeuvrable units designed to further unsettle us," he went on. "Your casualties will come from Corpsmen engaged on hull defence, personnel from the defending ships, and perhaps enemy casualties. Which brings me to a point which I would like cleared up. You seem to be handling a lot of enemy wounded, Doctor, and you've told me that your facilities are already strained to the limit . . ."

"How the blazes can you tell?" said Conway. Dermod's expression became more frigid, but this time he answered the question.

"Because I have reports of patients lying beside each other finding that the other one is talking gibberish, patients of the same physological type, that is. What steps are you taking to—"

"None!" said Conway, so angry suddenly that he wanted to take this cold, unfeeling martinet by the throat and shake some humanity into him.

At the beginning he had liked Dermod. He had thought him a thoughtful and sensitive as well as a competent fleet commander, but during the past few days he had become the embodiment of the blind, coldly implacable forces which had Conway and everyone else in the hospital trapped. Daily conferences between the military and medical authorities in the hospital had been ordered since the last attack had begun, and at all three of them Conway had found himself running across the fleet commander with increasing frequency.

But when Conway snapped, the fleet commander did not snap back. Dermod merely looked at him with his eyes so bleak and distant that Conway felt that the commander wasn't seeing him at all. And it did no good at all when O'Mara advised him quietly to hold his tongue and not be so all-fired touchy—that Dermod had a war to fight and he was doing the best he could, and that the pressures he was under excused a certain lack of charm in his personality.

"Surely," said Dermod coldly, just as Conway had decided that he really ought to be more patient with this cold-blooded, military creature, "you are not treating enemy casualties the same as our own . . .?"

"It is difficult," said Conway, speaking so quietly that O'Mara looked suddenly worried, "to tell the difference. Subtle variations in spacesuit design mean nothing to the nursing staff and myself. And when, as frequently happens, the suit and underlying uniform is cut away the latter may be unidentifiable due to the bleeding. Between the injection of antipain and unconsciousness the oral noises they make are not easily translatable. And if there is any way to tell the

144

difference between a Corpsman and one of the enemy screaming, I don't want to know about it . . ."

He had started quietly, but when he ended he was close to shouting.

". . . I won't make any such distinction between casualties and neither will my staff! This is a *hospital*, damn you! Well *isn't* it?"

"Take it easy, son. It's still a hospital," said O'Mara gently.

"It is also," Dermod snapped, "a military base!"

"What I don't understand," O'Mara put in quickly, trying desperately to pour on the oil, "is why the hell they don't finish us with atomic warheads . . . ?"

Another hit, more distant this time, sent its tinny echoes through the room.

"The reason they don't finish us off with an atomic bomb, Major," he replied, with his eyes still locked with Conway's, "is because they must make a conquest. The political forces involved demand it. The Empire must take and occupy this outpost of the hated enemy, the Emperor's general must have a triumph and not a pyrrhic victory, and subjugating the enemy and capturing his territory, no matter how few or how little, can be made to look like a triumph to the citizens of the Empire.

"Our own casualties are heavy," Dermod went on coldly. "A space battle being what it is only ten percent of the casualties survive to be hospitalised, and we are fortunate both in having medical facilities immediately available and in occupying a strong defensive position. The number of enemy casualties is much higher than ours, my estimate would be twenty to one, so that if they were to knock us out with an atomic missile now, when they could have done the same thing at the very beginning without losing a man, some very awkward questions will be asked within the Empire. If the Emperor can't answer them he might find that the war, and all the fine, martial fervour he has built up, will backfire on him . . ."

"Why don't you communicate with them?" Conway interrupted harshly. "Tell them the truth about us, and tell them about the wounded here. You surely don't expect to win this battle now. Why don't we surrender . . . ?"

"We cannot communicate with them, Doctor," the commander said bitingly, "because they won't listen to us. Or if they do listen they don't believe what we say. They know, or think they know, what we did on Etla and what we are supposed to be doing here. Telling them that we were really helping the Etlan natives and that we have been forced to defend our hospital is no good. A series of plagues swept Etla soon after we left and this establishment no longer behaves, outwardly, that is, like a hospital. What we say to them has no importance, it is what we *do* that counts. And we are doing exactly what their Emperor has lead them to expect of us.

"If they were really thinking," he continued savagely, "they would wonder at the large number of our e-ts who are helping us. According to them our e-ts are down-trodden, subject races who are little more than slaves. The volunteers who have come out to help us do not fight like slaves, but at the present stage that is too subtle a thing to make any impression. They are thinking emotionally instead of logically . . ."

"And *I'm* thinking emotionally, too!" Conway broke in sharply. "I'm thinking of my patients. The wards are full. They are lying in odd corners and along corridors all over the place, with inadequate protection against pressure loss . . ."

"You've lost the ability to think about anything *but* your patients, Doctor!" Dermod snapped back. "It might surprise you to know that I think about them, too, but I try not to be so mauldin about it. If I did think that way I would begin to feel angry, begin to hate the enemy. Before I know it I would want revenge . . ."

Another hit rang like a loud, discordant gong through the hospital. The commander raised his voice, and kept on raising it.

". . . You must know that the Monitor Corps is the police force for most of the inhabited Galaxy, and keeping the peace within the Federation for the constant application of the psychological and social sciences. In short, guiding and moulding opinion both on the individual and planetary population levels. So the situation we have here, a gallant band of Corpsmen and Doctors holding out against the savage, unceasing attacks of an overwhelmingly superior enemy, is one I could use. Even so it would take the Federation a long time to become angry enough to mobilise for war, far too long to do us personally any good, but think how we would be avenged, Doctor . . . !"

His voice was shaking now, his face white and tight with fury. He was shouting.

"In an interstellar war planets cannot be captured, Doctor. They can only be detonated. That stinking little Empire with its forty planets would be stamped out, destroyed, completely obliterated ... !"

O'Mara did not speak. Conway couldn't, nor could he take his eyes off Dermod to see how the psychologist was reacting to this outburst. He hadn't thought it possible for the commander to blow up like this and it was suddenly frightening. Because Dermod's sanity and self-control, like O'Mara's, was something Conway had depended on even though he hated it.

"But the Corps is a police force, remember?" he raged on. "We are trying to think of this as a disturbance, a riot on an interstellar scale where as usual the casualties among the rioters outnumber those of the police. Personally I think it is past the time when *anything* will make them see the truth and a full-scale war is inevitable, but I do not want to hate them. This is the difference, Doctor, between maintaining peace and waging war.

"And I don't want any snivelling, narrow-minded doctors, who have nothing to worry about except their patients, reminding me of all the horrible ways my men are dying. Trying to make me lose my perspective, making me hate people who are no different to us except that they are being fed wrong information.

"And I don't care if you treat enemy and Corps wounded alike," he yelled, trying to bring his voice down but not succeeding, "but you will listen when I give orders concerning them. This is a military base and they are enemy casualties. The ones who are in a condition to move must be guarded against the possibility of them committing acts of sabotage. Now do you understand, Doctor?"

"Yes, sir," said Conway in a small voice.

When he left Reception with O'Mara a few minutes later Conway still had the feeling of being charred around the edges. It was plain now that he had gravely misjudged the fleet commander, and he should apologise for the hard things he had been thinking about Dermod. Underneath all the ice Dermod was a good man.

Beside him O'Mara said suddenly, "I like to see these cold, controlled types blow off steam occasionally. Psychologically it is desirable, considering the pressures he is under at the present time. I'm glad you finally made him angry."

"What about *me*?" said Conway.

"You, Doctor, are not controlled at all," O'Mara replied sternly. "Despite your new authority, which should make you set an example of tolerance and good behavior at least, you are fast becoming a bad-tempered brat. Watch it, Doctor."

Conway had been looking for sympathy for the tongue-lashing Dermod had given him, and a little consideration for the pressures he himself was under, not criticism from another quarter. When O'Mara turned off towards his office a few minutes later, Conway was still too angry to speak.

## Chapter Twenty-Four

NEXT DAY Conway did not get the chance to apologise to the Fleet commander—the rioters launched their most vicious attack yet and both the Station Inspector and the Police Surgeon were much too busy to talk. But calling the battle a riot, Conway thought cynically, made no difference to the nature and number of the casualties which flooded suddenly in, because it began with a near-catastrophe for both sides.

The enemy force closed in, stepping up the missile bombardment to a fantastic rate and englobing the hospital so tightly that there were times when they came within a few hundred feet of the outer hull. Dermod's ships—Vespasian, a Tralthan capital ship and the other smaller units remaining to him—dropped back to anchor with tractors against the hospital, there being no space to manoeuvre without obstructing the heavy armament below them. They settled and with their lighter weapons strengthened the fixed defences wherever possible.

But this must have been the move which the enemy commander had been waiting for. With the rapidity possible only to a well-planned manoeuvre the ranks of the attacking globe thinned, scattered and reformed over one small area of the hull. On this area was concentrated the total firepower of three-quarters of the entire enemy force.

A storm of missiles tore into the heavy plating, blasting away the wreckage which plugged earlier damage and gouging into the more fragile inner hull. Tractors and rattlers seized the still-settling wreckage, shaking it viciously apart and pulling it away so that the missiles could gouge deeper still. Monitor defences took a frightful toll of the tightly packed ships, but only for minutes. The tremendous concentration of fire battered them down, hammered them flat, ripped and worried at them until they were one with the other shifting masses of savaged men and metal. They left a section of the outer hull completely undefended, and suddenly it became plain that this was not only an attack but an invasion.

Under the covering fire of the massed attackers, three, giant, unarmed ships were dropping ponderously towards the undefended section. Transports ...

At once *Vespasian* was directed to fill the gap in the defences. It shot towards the point where the first transport was about to touch down, running the gauntlet of Monitor as well as enemy fire and throwing everything it had as soon as the target appeared above the curve of the hull ...

There were several excuses given for what happened then. An error in judgment by its pilot, a hit by one of the enemy—or even its own people's—missiles which deflected it from course at exactly the wrong moment. But it was never suggested that Captain Williamson deliberately rammed the enemy transport, because Williamson was known to be a clear-headed, competent officer and a one-to-one swap, even at this desperate stage of the battle, was a tactically stupid move considering how the enemy outnumbered them.

*Vespasian* struck the larger but more lightly constructed transport near its stern and seemed to go right through it before grinding silently to a halt. Inside the wreckage a single, small explosion lit the fog of escaping air but the two ships remained locked together, spinning slowly.

For a second everything seemed to stop. Then the Monitor fixed defences lashed out, ignoring all other targets if their projectors would bear on the second descending transport. Within minutes rattlers had torn off plating in three areas of its hull and were biting deeper. The transport withdrew ponderously, losing air. The third one was already pulling back. The whole enemy force was pulling back, but not very far. Only slightly diminished in intensity the bombardment continued.

It was not by any stretch of the imagination a victory for the Monitor Corps. The enemy had merely made an error of judgment, been a little premature. The hospital required further softening up.

Tractor beams reached out and gently brought the spinning wreckage to a halt and lowered it onto the ravaged hull. Corpsmen jetted out to look for survivors and soon the casualties were coming in. But by roundabout routes, because under the wrecked ships there now stretched other wreckage and other rescue teams working to free patients who were casualties for the second and third time...

Dr. Prilicla was with the rescue teams. The GLNO lifeform was the most fragile known to the Federation, cowardice being acknowledged as one of their prime survival characteristics. But Prilicla was guiding his thin-walled pressure bubble over jagged plating and through wreckage which shifted visibly all around it, seeking life. Living minds radiated even when unconscious and the little GLNO was pointing out unerringly the living from the dead. With casualties bleeding to death inside their suits or the suits themselves losing pressure, such identification directed effort to where it did the most good, and Prilicla was saving many, many lives. But for an empath, an emotion sensitive, it was a hellish job in every horrible and painful sense of the word...

Major O'Mara was everywhere. If there hadn't been weightless conditions the Chief Psychologist would have been dragging himself from place to place, but as it was his extreme fatigue showed only in the way he misjudged distances and collided with doors and people. But when he talked to Earth-human patients, nurses and Corpsmen his voice was never tired. His mere presence had a steadying effect on the e-t staff as well, for although they could not understand him they remembered the person he had been when there were Translators and he could lift off their hides with a few pungent words.

The e-t staff—the massive, awkward Tralthan FGLIs, the crab-like Melfan ELNTs and all the others—were everywhere, on some levels directing Earth-human staff and on others aiding the nurses and Corpsmen orderlies. They were tired and harried and all too often they did not know what was being said to them, but between them they saved a great many lives.

And every time a missile struck the hospital, they lost a little ground . . .

Dr. Conway never left the dining hall. He had communication with most of the other levels, but the corridors leading to them were in many cases airless or blocked with wreckage, and it was the general opinion that the hospital's last remaining Senior Physician should stay in a reasonably safe place. He had plenty of human casualties to look after and the difficult e-t cases, whether combatants or casualties among his own staff, were sent to him.

In a way he had the biggest and most compact ward in the hospital. Since nobody had time to gather for meals anymore and relied on packaged food sent to the wards, the main dining hall had been converted. Beds and theatre equipment had been clamped to the floor, walls and ceiling of the great room and the patients, being space personnel, were not troubled either by the weightlessness or the sight of other patients hanging a few yards above them. It was convenient for the patients who were able to talk.

Conway had reached the stage of tiredness where he no longer felt tired. The tinny crash and clangour of missiles striking had become a monotonous background noise. He knew that the bombardment was steadily eating through the outer and inner hulls, a deadly erosion which must soon open every corridor and ward to space, but his brain had ceased to react to the sound. When casualties arrived he did what was indicated, but his reactions then were simply the conditioned reflexes of a doctor. He had lost much of his capacity to think or feel or remember, and when he did remember he had no sense of time. The last e-t case—which had required him taking four physiology tapes—stood out amid the weary, bloody, noisy monotony, as did the arrival of *Vespasian's* injured. But Conway did not know whether that had been three days or three weeks ago, or which incident had occurred first.

He remembered the *Vespasian* incident often. Cutting Major Stillman out of his battered suit, stripping it off and pushing away the pieces which persisted in floating around the bed. Stillman had two cracked ribs, a shattered humerus and a minor decompression which was temporarily affecting his

151

eye-sight. Until the hypo took hold he kept asking about the Captain.

And Captain Williamson kept asking about his men. Williamson was in a cast from neck to toes, had very little pain and had remembered Conway immediately. It had been a large crew and he must have known them all by their names. Conway didn't.

"Stillman is three beds away on your right," Conway had told him, "and there are others all over the place."

Williamson's eyes had moved along the patients hanging above him. He couldn't move anything else. "There's some of them I don't recognise," he had said.

Looking at the livid bruises around Williamson's right eye, temple and jaw where his face had struck the inside of his helmet, Conway had dragged up his mouth into the semblance of a smile and said, "Some of them won't recognise you."

He remembered the second TRLH . . .

It had arrived strapped to a pressure litter whose atmosphere unit had already filled it with the poison which the occupant called air. Through the twin transparencies of the litter wall and the TRLH's suit its injuries were plainly apparent—a large, depressed fracture of the carapace which had cut underlying blood vessels. There was no time to take the tapes he had used during the previous TRLH case because the patient was obviously bleeding to death. Conway nodded for the litter to be clamped into the cleared area in the centre of the floor and quickly changed his suit gauntlets for litter gloves. From the beds attached to the ceiling, eyes watched his every move.

He charged the gloves and pushed his hands against the sagging, transparent fabric of the tent. Immediately the thin, tough material became rubbery and pliable without losing any of its strength. It clung to the charged gloves, if not like a second skin at least like another pair of thin gloves. Carefully so as not to strain the fabric which separated the two mutually poisonous atmospheres, Conway removed the patient's suit with instruments clipped to the inside of the litter.

Quite complex procedures were possible while operating a flexible tent—Conway had a couple of PVSJs and a QCQL a few beds away to prove it—but they were limited by the instruments and medication available inside the tent, and the slight hampering effect of the fabric.

He had been removing the splinters of carapace from the damaged area when the crash of a missile striking nearby made the floor jump. The alarm bell which indicated a pressure drop sounded a few minutes later and Murchison and the Kelgian military doctor—the entire ward staff—had hurried to check the seals on the tents of patients who were not able to check their own. The drop was slight, probably a small leak caused by sprung plating, but to Conway's patient inside the tent it could be deadly. He had begun working with frantic speed.

But while he had striven to tie off the severed blood vessels the thin, tough fabric of the pressure litter began to swell out. It had become difficult to hold instruments, virtually impossible to guide them accurately, and his hands were actually pushed away from the operative field. The difference in pressure between the interior of the tent and the ward was only a few pounds per square inch at most, barely enough to have made Conway's ears pop, but the fabric of the litter had continued to balloon out. He had withdrawn helplessly, and half an hour later when the leak had been sealed and normal pressure restored, he had started again. By then it had been too much.

He remembered a sudden impairment of vision then, and a shock of surprise when he realised that he was crying. Tears weren't a conditioned medical reflex, he knew, because doctors just did not cry over patients. Probably it had been a combination of anger at losing the patient—who really should not have been lost—and his extreme fatigue. And when he'd seen the expressions of all the patients watching him, Conway had felt horribly embarrassed.

Now the events around him had taken on a jerky, erratic motion. His eyes kept closing and several seconds, or minutes, passed before he could force them open again even though to himself no time at all went by. The walking wounded—patients with injuries which allowed them to move about the ward and return quickly to their tents in the event of a puncture—were moving from bed to bed doing the small, necessary jobs, or chatting with patients who couldn't move, or hanging like ungainly shoals of fish while they talked among themselves. But Conway was always too busy with the newly-arrived patients, or too confused with a multiplicity of

153

tapes, to chat with the older ones. Mostly, however, his eyes went to the sleeping figures of Murchison and the Kelgian who floated near the entrance to the ward.

The Kelgian hung like a great, furry question mark, now and then emitting the low moaning sound which some DBLFs made when they were asleep. Murchison floated at the end of a snaking, ten-foot safety line, turning slowly. It was odd how sleepers in the weightless condition adopted the foetal position, Conway thought tenderly as he watched his beautiful, adult, girl baby swaying at the end of an impossibly thin umbilical cord. He desperately wanted to sleep himself, but it was his spell on duty and he would not be relieved for a long time—five minutes maybe, or five hours, but an eternity in either case. He would have to keep doing something.

Without realising he had made a decision he found himself moving into the empty storeroom which housed the terminal and probable terminal cases. It was only here that Conway spared himself the time to chat, or if talking was not possible to do the essential and at the same time useless things which help to comfort the dying. With the e-ts he could only stand by and hope that the shattered, bloody wreckage of the Tralthan or Melfan or whatever would be given a tiny flash of Prilicla's emphathetic faculty so that they would know he was a friend and how he felt.

It was only gradually that Conway became aware that the walking wounded had followed him into the room, together with patients who had no business being outside their tents who were being towed by the others. They gathered slowly around and above him, their expression grim, determined and respectful. Major Stillman pushed his way to the front, awkwardly, because in his one good hand he carried a gun.

"The killing has got to stop, Doctor," Stillman said quietly. "We've all talked it over and that's what we decided. And it's got to be stopped right now." He reversed the weapon suddenly, offering it to Conway. "You might need this, to point at Dermod to keep him from doing anything foolish while we're telling him what has been going on..."

Close behind Stillman hung the mummified shape of Captain Williamson and the man who had towed him in. They were talking to each other in low voices and the language was both foreign and familiar to Conway. Before he could place it the patients all began moving out again and he noticed how many of them were armed. The weapons had been part of the spacesuits they had worn, and Conway had not thought about guns when he had piled the suits into a ward storage space. Dermod, he thought, would be very annoyed with him. Then he followed the patients out to the main ward entrance, and the corridor which led to Reception.

Stillman talked nearly all the time, telling him what had been happening. When they were almost there he said anxiously, "You don't think I'm . . . I'm a traitor for doing this, Doctor?"

There were so many different emotions churning inside Conway that all he could say was *"No!"*

# Chapter Twenty-Five

HE FELT ridiculous pointing the gun at the Fleet commander, but that had seemed to be the only way to do this thing. Conway had entered Reception, threaded his way through the officers around the control desks until he had reached Dermod, then he had held the gun on the fleet commander while the others came in. He had also tried to explain things, but he wasn't doing a very good job.

". . . So you want me to surrender, Doctor," said Dermod wearily, not looking at the gun. His eyes went from Conway's face to those of some of the Corpsmen patients who were still floating into the room. He looked hurt and disappointed, as if a friend had done a very shameful thing.

Conway tried again.

"Not surrender, sir," he said, pointing at the man who was still guiding Williamson's stretcher. "We . . . I mean, that man over there needs a communicator. He wants to order a cease fire . . ."

Stammering in his eagerness to explain what had happened, Conway started with the influx of casualties after the collision between *Vespasian* and the enemy transport. The interiors of both ships were a shambles and, while it was known that there were enemy as well as Corpsmen injured, there had never been time or the staff available to separate them. Then

155

later, when the less seriously injured began to move around, talking to or helping to nurse the other patients, it became plain that almost half of the casualties were from the other side. Oddly this did not seem to matter much to the patients, and the staff were too busy to notice. So the patients went on doing the simpler, necessary and not very pleasant jobs for each other, jobs which just had to be done in a ward so drastically understaffed, and talking . . .

For these were Corpsmen from *Vespasian*, and *Vespasian* had been to Etla. Which meant that its crew were variously proficient in the Etlan language, and the Etlans spoke the same language as that used all over the Empire—a general purpose language similar to the Federation's Universal. They talked to each other a lot and one of the things they learned, after the initial caution and distrust had passed, was that the enemy transport had contained some very high officers. One of the ones who had survived the collision was third in line of command of the Empire forces around Sector General . . .

". . . And for the last few days peace talks have been going on among my patients," Conway ended breathlessly. "Unofficial, perhaps, but I think Colonel Williamson and Heraltnor here have enough rank to make them binding."

Heraltnor, the enemy officer, spoke briefly and vehemently to Williamson in Etlan, then gently tilted the plaster encased figure of the Captain until he could look at the fleet commander. Heraltnor watched Dermod, too. Anxiously.

"He's no fool, sir," said Williamson painfully. "From the sound of the bombardment and the glimpses he's had of your screens he knows our defences are hammered flat. He says that his people could land now and we couldn't do a thing to stop them. That is true, sir, and we both know it. He says his chief will probably order the landing in a matter of hours, but he still wants a cease fire, sir, not a surrender.

"He doesn't want his side to win," the Captain ended weakly. "He just wants the fighting to stop. There are some things he has been told about this war and us which need straightening out, he says . . ."

"He's been saying a lot," said Dermod angrily. His face had a tortured look, as if he was wanting desperately to hope but did not dare let himself do so. He went on, "And you men have been doing a lot of talking! Why didn't you let me know about it . . ?"

"It wasn't what we *said*," Stillman broke in sharply, "it

156

was what we *did!* They didn't believe a word we told them at first. But this place wasn't at all what they had been told to expect, it looked more like a hospital than a torture chamber. Appearances could have been deceptive, and they were a very suspicious bunch, but they saw human and e-t doctors and nurses working themselves to death over them, and they saw *him.* Talking didn't do anything, at least not until later. It was what we did, what *he* did . . . !"

Conway felt his ears getting warm. He protested, "But the same thing was happening in every ward of the hospital!"

"Shut up, Doctor," Stillman said respectfully, then went on, "He never seemed to sleep. He hardly ever spoke to us once we were out of danger, but the patients in the side ward he never let up on, even though they were the hopeless cases. A couple of them he proved not to be hopeless, and moved them out to us in the main ward. It didn't matter what side they were on, he worked as hard for everybody . . ."

"Stillman," said Conway sharply, "you're dramatising things . . . !"

". . . Even then they were wavering a bit," Stillman went on regardless. "But it was the TRLH case which clinched things. The TRLHs were enemy e-t volunteers, and normally the Empire people don't think much of e-ts and expected us to feel the same. Especially as this e-t was on the other side. But he worked just as hard on it, and when the pressure drop made it impossible for him to go on with the operation and the e-t died, they saw his reaction—"

*"Stillman!"* said Conway furiously.

But Stillman did not go into details. He was silent, watching Dermod anxiously. Everybody was watching Dermod. Except Conway, who was looking at Heraltnor.

The Empire officer did not look very impressive at that moment, Conway thought. He looked like a very ordinary, greying, middle-aged man with a heavy chin and worry-lines around his eyes. In comparison to Dermod's trim green uniform with its quietly impressive load of insignia the shapeless, white garment issued to DBDG patients put Heraltnor at somewhat of a disadvantage. As the silence dragged on Conway wondered whether they would salute each other or just nod.

But they did better than either, they shook hands.

There was an initial period of suspicion and mistrust, of

course. The Empire commander-in-chief was convinced that Heraltnor had been hypnotised at first, but when the investigating party of Empire officers landed on Sector General after the cease fire the distrust diminished rapidly to zero. For Conway the only thing which diminished was his worries regarding wards being opened to space. There was still too much for his staff and himself to do, even though engineers and medical officers from the Empire fleet were doing all they could to put Sector General together again. While they worked the first trickle of the evacuated staff began to return, both medical and maintenance, and the Translator computer went back into operation. Then five weeks and six days after the cease fire the Empire fleet left the vicinity of the hospital. They left their wounded behind them, the reasons being that they were getting the best possible treatment where they were, and that the fleet might have more fighting to do.

In one of the daily meetings with the hospital authorities —which still consisted of O'Mara and Conway since nobody more senior to them had come with the recent arrivals —Dermod tried to put a complex situation into very simple terms.

"... Now that the Imperial citizens know the truth about Etla among other things," he said seriously, "the Emperor and his administration are virtually extinct. But things are still very confused in some sectors and a show of force will help stabilise things. I'd like it to be just a show of force, which is why I talked their commander into taking some of our cultural contact and sociology people with him. We want rid of the Emperor, but not at the price of a civil war.

"Heraltnor wanted you to go along, too, Doctor. But I told him that..."

Beside him O'Mara groaned. "Besides saving hundreds of lives," the Chief Psychologist said, "and averting a galaxy-wide war, our miracle-working, brilliant young doctor is being called on to—"

"Stop needling him, O'Mara!" Dermod said sharply. "Those things are literally true, or very nearly so. If he hadn't..."

"Just force of habit, sir," said O'Mara blandly. "As a head-shrinker I consider it my bounden duty to keep his from swelling..."

At that moment the main screen behind Dermod's desk, manned by a Nidian Receptionist now instead of a Monitor officer, lit with a picture of a furry Kelgian head. It appeared that there was a large DBLF transport coming in with FGLI and ELNT staff aboard in addition to the Kelgians, eighteen of which were Senior Physicians. Bearing in mind the damaged state of the hospital and the fact that just three locks were in operable condition, the Kelgian on the screen wanted to discuss quarters and assignments *before* landing with the Diagnostician-in-Charge...

"Thornnastor's still unfit and there are no other..." Conway began to say when O'Mara reached across to touch his arm.

"Seven tapes, remember," he said gruffly. "Let us not quibble, Doctor."

Conway gave O'Mara a long, steady look, a look which went deeper than the blunt, scowling features and the sarcastic, hectoring voice. Conway was not a Diagnostician—what he had done two months ago had been forced on him, and it had nearly killed him. But what O'Mara was saying —with the touch of his hand and the expression in his eyes, not the scowl on his face and the tone of his voice—was that it would be just a matter of time.

Colouring with pleasure, which Dermod probably put down to embarrassment at O'Mara's ribbing, he dealt quickly with the quartering and duties of the staff on the Kelgian transport, then excused himself. He was supposed to meet Murchison at the recreation level in ten minutes, and she had asked *him*...

As he was leaving he heard O'Mara saying morosely, "...And in addition to saving countless billions from the horrors of war, I bet he gets the girl, too..."